UNTOUCHABLE GIRL

FAÎTE FALLING
BOOK SIX

MARY E. TWOMEY

Untouchable Girl
Book Six in the Faîte Falling Series

By

Mary E. Twomey

COPYRIGHT

DEDICATION

*Special thanks to all the teachers who never gave up on me,
namely Mr. Richard Grieves.*

*And for those of you who did,
I super don't blame you.
I was a pill.*

1

THE LONGEST TWO WEEKS OF MY LIFE

I don't care what anyone tells you, two weeks is an eternity to wait for your mom to come home to you. Lane had been gone for so long already, searching out allies in the withering provinces and inviting them to share in our newfound wealth. Stealing half the jewels back from Morgan was a scandal no one took lightly. Refugees from all over Avalon were still pouring in to stake their claims on a plot of land that wasn't under Morgan le Fae's rule.

Bastien was still gone, and if Kerdik hadn't magicked the castle to keep me locked inside, I would've gone along to help free Lane, Damond, Reyn, Remy, and... My fragile optimism always waned on that last one. The thought of Judah being held in a dungeon was a mental image I couldn't deal with if I wanted to keep my sanity. Judah had been my favorite (and often only) friend from grade school on, and deserved the best out of life. I'm talking parades, scholarships, hip-hop songs rapped in his honor – the works. What he did not deserve was to get caught up in my mess, and land himself smack in the middle of my mom's dungeon, without his glasses, and without me. I could picture him huddling in a corner with Lane, scared and cold. The image woke me up in the middle of the night, wracking me with fear. Then came the crash of self-loathing when I remembered I couldn't break myself out of the castle and go get him myself.

I frowned when a knock came to my bedroom door. I knew it was Kerdik, and I was still miffed at him for cutting me off from the rescue team. I took my sweet time opening the door, and shot daggers at him with my eyes when he greeted me with an irritable expression. "Took you long enough."

"If I haven't told you before, your personality is absolutely bursting with fruit flavor." I rolled my eyes at him, my hand on my hip. "Are you here to check that I haven't made an escape rope out of old sheets and flung them out the window, Warden?"

"If you were capable of besting my spellwork, then that's exactly what I'd be doing. As you can't even step a toe out of the castle, I'm not too concerned. I've brought you a friend to help you sleep."

The raccoon in his arms was grousing worse than me, and looked about an inch from biting into Kerdik's juicy forearm just to have done with it. "Hey, Walter," I greeted him without enthusiasm. Walter was a sourpuss, who had nothing good to say about the world. Montel wasn't too keen on me sleeping with another bear, so he thought a smaller animal would be best. Walter was a bit of a jerk, though, and we spent most of our time being pissed at each other. Then when I was certain he'd heard me, but was just ignoring me, I repeated myself with a little extra cheeriness. "I said, 'Hey, Walter.'"

"Do you really need to talk all the time?"

"Well, seeing as how that's what you're here for, yes."

"You're exhausting."

I sighed up at Kerdik. "Remind me again why I can't just have my birds? They'll knock me out so much quicker with all their chatter."

"Because the Sluagh can change himself into a raven. We can't chance him mingling with the other birds and flying his way straight inside."

"Still no sign of the Grim Reaper, eh?" A Sluagh was a wicked person who'd died, and his spirit was so evil that a Sluagh was formed. The nasty bugger roams about, trying to suck the souls from the dying, adding to its power with each conquest. As I understood it, these jaggoffs were usually only in Éireland, but this dude made a special trip overseas just for Madigan. The Sluagh was targeting me now, courtesy of my fake engagement to Mad.

Kerdik sighed at my appearance. "What are you wearing?"

I looked down and rolled up the sleeves of the shirt

that hung down almost to my knees. "What? I'm allowed to wear my boyfriend's flannel shirts as pajamas. They're comfortable. I can look however I want in my own bedroom."

Kerdik's disapproving expression wasn't all that uncommon this week. He always had a bug up his butt about something. "I don't like the look of you in his clothes. Have Montel and Link seen you like this?"

"Of course not. Link prefers me in nothing at all, so that's how I greet him every morning."

Kerdik pursed his lips, unamused by my pretty funny joke. "Hilarious."

I crossed my arms over my chest and moved over to my window, unwilling to play this game for a third night in a row. "I'm sorry you can't find the Sluagh. I know you get moody when you lose."

He stood straighter, affronted. "I didn't lose. I'll find the Sluagh and make it suffer for forcing me to run around like a Commoner, searching for his own tail."

"Ugh. This guy. He's so annoying."

"Hush, Walter. Kerdik's just in a mood."

Kerdik's shoulders were tight as he stalked over to me. "I despise when you talk about me as if I'm a child."

"If you don't want to be treated like a child, then stop acting like a petulant baby."

Kerdik let out a noise of frustration. "You drive me crazy!"

"Me? You're the one who locked me inside, when I

could be helping Bastien and the guys find Lane. At the very least, I could be helping the crew build the wall."

"I have half a mind to raise up the rest of the wall myself, just to have done with it."

I gaped at him. "Could you really do that?"

He shot me a simpering expression. "You must be joking."

I ran my fingers over Walter's fur, and he hissed for me to knock it off. "I guess that never dawned on me."

"Oh, sweet girl. Your mind is so limited when it comes to all I can do."

I scowled at him, looking more like the surly Walter than a girl should have a right to. "Don't call me 'sweet girl' when you're really saying 'you dummy'. It's patronizing." When we reached our usual nostril-flaring stalemate, I lowered my shoulders and fished for a lighter topic. "Where's Montel?"

"Doing a perimeter check before he turns in to sleep."

Montel was a nervous sleeper, which wasn't helped by the fact that Link made a big deal the first night about no man sharing a bed with an Untouchable's woman. I wasn't going to invite Montel into my bed in the first place, but the air had gone awkward all the same. "Okay. Did you need something?"

"A lock of your hair, actually."

I quirked my eyebrow at him. "Come again?"

He gave me a labored sigh, as if my simple query was an arduous give-me-a-break. "Do you really want the complicated explanation, or can I just say that it'll help me find the Sluagh, and be done with it?"

"If I'm donating body parts, I think I'll request the complicated explanation."

A labored sigh escaped his lips, complete with an eyeroll. "Every now and then, I wish you were afraid of me, like everyone else is. Then I wouldn't have to do taxing things, like explain myself." Kerdik harrumphed, as if my request was a huge inconvenience. "The Sluagh found you in Avalon, even though he's from Éireland. I want to know if it's you he's tracking now, or if it's still Madigan he's after. If he's tracking you, I can use the line of magic he's tapping to trace it back to him."

"Huh. Okay, then that's cool. See? Was that so hard to tell me?" I cast around for scissors, but didn't see any.

Kerdik pulled a pair from his back pocket. They were long and looked more like shears for sheep or something, which I guess it's possible they were. He made his way over to me and inspected my hair, as if one chunk would be more ideal for the magic than the others. "This one," he said, lifting up a curl to examine. It was a perfect Shirly Temple curl, unadulterated by a hairbrush or life. I didn't have a ton of perfect curls, but guessed donating one of them to save my life wouldn't be too grand a sacrifice. He pulled a string from the pocket of his standard brown pressed trousers and tied off the curl at the root. "Hold still."

The look on Kerdik's face when he examined my hair

in his hand made me soften, feeling things I wasn't prepared to put words to. He snipped the curl, not taking his eyes from the milk chocolate color I'd long been unimpressed by. Seeing my hair through his eyes was a new wonder, and I appreciated afresh that there were parts of me that were beautiful. I'd been the stupid and ugly girl most of my life. The little looks of rapture that Kerdik or Bastien often shot me still took me off-guard.

A soft smile played on my lips. "Thank you."

Kerdik quirked his eyebrow at me. "For taking your hair? You're welcome?"

"No, for looking at it like that. Made me feel pretty just then."

Kerdik chuckled, and I loved the way his eyes crinkled in the corners only for me. Something about the green skin made the delicate folds that much more intriguing. "Well, you are pretty, so I'm not sure I did anything miraculous, other than notice what's right in front of my face."

"Just mate already and be done with it," Walter sneered.

We stood before each other, the heat rising and falling, as it always did. I was with Bastien now, so I did my best to keep things platonic, which was most likely why Kerdik was so crabby these past two weeks. "Sorry the hunt for this jag is trickier than you'd hoped. I know you've got more important things to do than this."

"I can't think of a one." He reached out and stroked a curl that framed my face, addressing it instead of me when he spoke. "I'll be expecting a hero's song from you when I find this Sluagh who's proved so problematic."

"Something with a ragtime downbeat that ends in 'Kerdik's the King!' sound good?" I did a goofy flapper-style dance for him, which seemed to break the perpetual sexual tension. What can I say? I'm a very gifted dancer.

He opened his mouth to respond, but the knock on the door interrupted our back and forth. Kerdik motioned with his hand, using his elemental gift to blow the door open, startling me and Montel, who was on the other side. "Good evening, Princess," Montel said with his chin lowered. Everyone was on their best behavior around Kerdik.

"Hey, man. No sign of Notorious B.A.D.?"

"None at all, your grace. I'll need to check your windows before I turn in. I can ask your father or your handmaidens to come up while I secure your window, if you prefer."

Montel was precious, giving respect for the fact that he was a man entering a woman's room, instead of just barging in. It was nice to be treated like a lady, after everything I'd experienced in Avalon. "No worries. Come on in." Montel waited in the doorway until I waved him forward.

Speaking of barging in, Link's voice carried up the steps, greeting me before his smile strolled into the room. "Rosie, I love ye. Rosie, I care. Rosie, without ye, my heart's in despair." He paused his song to stretch his arms over his head. "I defeated him, the lousy codger. With one hand tied behind my back, I flattened his ugly gob. Where's my parade? Jays, woman! Where are the loose lasses, throwing themselves at their brave hero?"

I bounced on the balls of my feet with new hope. "You found the Sluagh? You killed him?"

Link's shoulders fell. "Nah. I was only joking. I don't know why I thought tha would be funny." He scratched his head, and then double-checked the window Montel had just secured.

Kerdik was never in the mood for Link's jokes, so he pretended they didn't exist. "I'll need to be away for the night." He held up my hair to show the guys. "I have what I need for the tracking spell I was telling you about, but I won't know if it works if I'm in the room with Rosie. I need to take her hair far away, to see if I can lure him there." He moved to the window – now the third guy who thought the Sluagh would come in by way of a third-floor narrow glass opening. Once Kerdik was satisfied with my security, he shut the drapes. "You'll leave these closed, even in the daytime. It won't do for me to set the perfect trap, pretending you're off far away, and the Sluagh taking a look at you and knowing it's all a setup."

"Fair enough." I moved over to my wardrobe and pulled out a pair of jeans I slid on under Bastien's shirt. I had been ready for bed, but now it looked like there might be men in and out of my bedroom for a while.

"Why are there so many people here? I usually only have to put up with your mouth," Walter whined.

"I can spread word that the princess is traveling through the province, if that helps," Montel offered.

Kerdik shrugged. "It couldn't hurt. And I don't want her sleeping here anymore."

I crossed my arms, my lips in a tight line. "You're doing that thing again. Whenever you go into bossypants mode, you talk about me like I'm not in the room."

"Fine. Darling, I don't want you sleeping here anymore. This is a westward-facing room. Sluaghs always enter through the west entrances. I can't believe it only just dawned on me this evening. We should've had you in a different room from the start."

"Okay, but with the rumor going around that I'm not here, that means I can't hold court with my dad. I don't like that I'm not with him, and neither is Draper. We were a team, and I feel like I'm leaving him hanging out to dry."

Kerdik smiled at me, as if my concerns were adorable. "Urien was ruling long before you were alive, my love. He'll miss you by his side, but he can handle the mundane squabbles of the people. Though, having a man on the throne without a woman to sanction everything is most unorthodox. I'll talk to him about it before I leave." Then before I could tell him my next concern, he said, "And I'll make sure his security's tightened before I go. I know how you worry about him, as though he's the child and you're the parent."

"Well, he's fragile. He only just woke up from a two-decade slumber."

"He says he's fine. Strong as ever."

"Yeah, well, I caught him yawning the other day. He's burning through his magic, helping everyone how he does while he's still just coming back to life. I don't want him overdoing it."

Kerdik stroked his knuckle down my cheekbone, gazing at me as if I was something special. "I love that you worry yourself about the safety of my dearest friend."

Whenever it dawned on me that I'd made out with my dad's bestie, I tried to suppress a grimace. Kerdik didn't look super old, but that didn't change reality. "Can I talk to him before I hole myself up in a non-westward-facing room?"

Kerdik clicked his fingers at Montel, silently telling him to go fetch my dad for me. I didn't like how much of a tyrant Kerdik was, or that a strong dude like Montel didn't even take offense at the rude ordering around. When Montel left, Kerdik spoke to Link without looking at him. "Pack up my queen's things and move them to the largest room on the other side of the castle. Preferably a room with no windows."

Link didn't argue, but he cast me a look that told me he didn't much care for being bossed. He and I started packing up my clothes quietly.

"Servants handle that, Rosie. You don't move your things. Link can do it."

"Link's my friend, and an Untouchable. He's no one's servant."

Kerdik tweaked my nose. "Everyone is your servant, because I say so. You're their princess, but you're my queen. Never forget that. Let him do his job; I need to speak with you in private."

When Link stomped out with two armloads of my clothes, I sank heavily onto the bed, pulling my knees to my chest as I sat on the edge of the mattress. "I sincerely hope you didn't just get all my clothes dunked in the mud or something. You're going to piss people off, being a jag like that." I folded my hands over my shins. "You're a little tightly wound today. You want to talk about what's making you be such a tool?"

Kerdik paced next to my bed, his brows pushed together in thought. "The last time I left for a long while, you were found starved and naked at the bottom of a well. No matter how powerful I am, it seems Morgan will always find a way to snatch at the people I love. If not Morgan, then Cailleach will do the job." He sat down on the edge of the bed. "Do you know much about Link's land?"

"Not really. Sluagh's come from there, so I'm guessing it's not a place I'd want to live."

"Cailleach is their *me*, to put it simply. The people of Éireland fear and obey the immortal sisters – Cailleach and Brìghde – as Avalon does me, only they're a little more beloved than I am."

"I don't see how that's possible. You're such a snuggly bunny," I teased.

"Ha. You aren't the first to think so." His hint was left in the air between us. I kept my body as motionless as possible, sensing there was more. I waited for him to open up, worried what might happen if he kept himself a secret forever, but worried more at what darkness might come spilling out when he finally opened his mouth.

THE BIRDS, THE BEES AND THE DRAGON

Kerdik stared at one of the posts on my bed, admiring the errant angel wings that had been carved into the honey-colored wood. "Do you know of Cailleach Bheur?"

"I can't say I do. Why don't you tell me about him or her." I shifted and leaned back on my pillows, settling in for what I hoped would be a good bedtime story. Walter crawled onto my chest, grumbling that my breasts weren't the right consistency for a nest. I ran my fingers over his fur to soothe his crabbiness as I waited for Kerdik to open up.

"Cailleach Bheur has just as much power as I do, only it's focused in different areas. Where I can do a lot with the water and earth elements, she does a lot with weather. They call her the Winter Queen, which is quite the fitting title. She sees to half the year in Éireland, killing off the insects and diseases during the winter, which keeps Éire-land thriving. Spring is controlled by her dear sister, Brìghde."

"That's sweet that they work together, keeping tight as a family."

Kerdik shot me a look, letting me know "sweet" wasn't the right word. "Long ago, maybe a handful of years before you were born, I traveled to Éireland to see if I could acquire a few of their abilities. I can affect the weather with my moods, sure, but I can't do it on purpose. I didn't know if that skill could be taught."

"And now you're the most awesome gangsta of all?" I smiled over at him, stroking Walter's tail.

"Not hardly. As it turns out, the gift can't be taught. The sisters are fairly stingy on sharing their talents." His tone turned guilty. "However, that wasn't the only purpose of my visit. I may or may not have spent a little alone time with Brìghde."

I smirked at him, glad he was spilling his guts. "Sly dog." Then I stiffened. "Wait, but what about your curse? If you sleep with a woman, she turns into a dragon. Is that what happened to Brìghde? She's some immortal, weather-controlling springtime dragon? Because... yikes."

He straightened the cuffs on his pressed white shirt, and smoothed his palm down his charcoal three-button vest, as if that would make his sexual history go away. "Not entirely. I was impulsive back then. Much to Cailleach's dismay, I seduced her sister, who's always been fairly impetuous. Brìghde was married back then, and our little affair sort of ended their union."

I let out a low whistle. "Jeez. You take the immortal bit out of that, and you've got your own talk show fodder."

"Brìghde didn't turn into a dragon because that all happened before I was cursed." He looked down, his gaze hard and his mouth in a tight line. "Cailleach was furious that I'd broken her sister's heart. She made it so that anyone I coupled with would turn into a dragon. Brìghde's the last woman I laid with who didn't."

I didn't know what to say to that. "I'm so sorry. Seems like a rough retaliation, and entirely one-sided. I mean Brìghde cheated willingly, right? Cailleach aimed her fire in the wrong direction."

"Exactly. I wasn't at fault."

When a cloudy red wave started to pollute the pure green of Kerdik's skin, I recoiled. "You're lying! I can see your lies, remember? You were totally at fault, and you know it."

"Wonderful. This is so inconvenient," he grumbled, and then sighed. "I may have put it in Brìghde's head that I would be around if she left her husband, but I had no intention of doing so." Kerdik kept his head down. "I went to see Brìghde again when I fell in love with Tara, a few years later. I apologized and begged her to get Cailleach to take back the curse. She said that if I gave her some of my magic, she would. So I gave her the ability to add more heat to her springtime, giving them summer – a concoction I'd meddled with over the years. My fire ability has always been stronger than hers. It added to her springtime, and makes for a pleasant summer in Éireland." He bit down on his lower lip and closed his eyes for a brief moment. I could tell he was in the throes of hating himself.

I moved Walter off my chest and sat up, scooting across the bed so I could sit next to Kerdik. My feet dangled over the edge of the bed, and I looped my arm through his, so he didn't have to feel so alone. "Then what happened?"

"She took my gift, and told me my curse was lifted. Only it wasn't. I made love to Tara, and she mutated in the middle of our coupling, turning my sweet girlfriend into a monster even she couldn't live with. Brìghde got Tara killed." He shook his head at himself. "I shouldn't have trusted her forgiveness. That was my foolish mistake. *I* got Tara killed."

Kerdik's fist clenched, so I worked my fingers around his knuckles to gently pry them open, lest the whole castle start shaking with his poorly bottled rage. "Tell me about Tara. What was she like?"

"She wasn't afraid of me," he stated simply, as if that was all it took for him to fall in love. "She looked at my skin as if I was a masterpiece, not a leper. She was good to me." His face moved from rhapsodical to sour. "She was good to me, and I turned her into a monster."

"It's not that simple. You tried to make things right with Brìghde. You thought the curse was broken."

Kerdik made a noncommittal grunt, but that was all he

would concede on the matter. "I won't make that mistake again. I won't have sex with anyone else until I'm certain my curse is completely lifted."

I wanted to point out that we'd finally managed to kiss without pyrotechnics, but realized that wasn't exactly proof the curse was completely gone. Kerdik was protecting me, and I respected that.

Kerdik swallowed hard, and then continued, looking off to the side. "The Hemlock that was used to put Urien into his slumber? It was pure, unadulterated by time or crosspollination of crops. To be that potent while still non-volatile, the Hemlock would have to be a first-generation plant. The only way I can think that would be possible is for Morgan to have gone to Brìghde, begging her to grow her a new plant. Brìghde can do that, just as I can. I know I didn't produce any Hemlock for Morgan to stumble across; it had to have been her."

"You think Brìghde has it in for my dad because you love him?"

Kerdik nodded. "It's what I'm afraid of, yes. Immortals hold grudges long after they should've been forgotten. Our fury is one of the few things that stays constant, as the rest of the world mutates with time around us."

I closed my eyes to fend off my frustration. "Great. How long have you known about this?"

"I still don't *know*. I only suspect. I'm only telling you because I worry about your safety. If she hears of my love for you, and sees that I'm not going to lose control and turn you into a dragon, I'm afraid she'll take matters into her own hands. She'll come after you, Rosie. That's why I need you to stay in the house while I'm gone."

"You didn't give me much choice," I replied with a small smile. "You locked me inside the castle, goof."

"And as much as you despise me for it, I won't risk your safety. You're their princess, but you're *my* queen. Brìghde is cunning. She'll do anything to destroy what I love, since she can't destroy me. Immortals don't go for the gut; they go for the heart." He laced his fingers through mine and squeezed as he glanced at me out of the corner of his eye. "And you, my darling, are my heart."

I knew this was the part where I normally would've kissed his cheek, but I was trying to avoid stepping out on Bastien, now that we were actually together. Though a cheek kiss could be innocent with anyone else, everything was dangerous with Kerdik. Instead I leaned my head on his shoulder, and cuddled into him when his arm found its way around my hips. "I feel like I should be freaking out that a vengeful immortal might have beef with me, but honestly, what's one more crazy log to throw on the fire? Promise you'll be careful while you're gone, trying to draw the Sluagh away?"

"See? Only you would worry about my safety when I warn you about danger that might be headed your way. That's only one of the many reasons I adore you." He kissed the top of my head as he held me on the side of the bed. "Sluaghs are no real threat to me. More annoyingly slippery than anything else. I'll deal with this last one, and come straight home to you, so you can fawn over me, as if I was mortal and had been in real danger."

When my father cleared his throat from the doorway, I looked up to find his expression tight and displeased. "Is there a reason you're making yourself at home on my daughter's bed?" he accused Kerdik.

"Kerdik's my friend," I declared, setting the record straight for all of us – including myself. "Hey, Dad. How goes working solo tonight?"

"It's lonely, but I'd rather you're safe up here. Kerdik's right about the westward-facing rooms. We haven't had Sluaghs in Avalon before, so I didn't even think of that. I'm a little rusty on my knowledge of Éireland's magic, I admit. But one rule that's held true through the years is that the bad creatures must be cast out, so that's what we've set in our minds to do, once we come across this Sluagh again."

Kerdik stood and faced his friend. "I'm taking off to try and lure the Sluagh from the castle using a lock of Rosie's hair and a *chasse* charm."

"Thank you. When you come back, you can use one of the many other rooms in my home to stay in. You'll meet with Rosie in one of the receiving rooms, as is proper."

I raised my eyebrow at my dad. "Sounds like you've had a long day. You're extra crabby. You want to talk about it?"

My dad's shoulders fell slightly, his barreled chest deflating. "It has been long. I didn't expect to be without Lane still. There are things about Avalon now that I'm expected to fix, but can't seem to. They trust a woman on the throne more than a man who's been out of touch for far too long. I'm afraid I'm still catching up."

"I'll leave you to your father," Kerdik said quietly, casting me a smirk at being treated like the bad boy coming to call on the virgin for nothing but naughty reasons. He made to kiss my lips, but I turned my chin, offering my cheek instead. He brushed his lips to my heated skin and whispered, "Always teasing me, leaving me wanting more. Of all the Fae I've met, you hold the most power over me."

I blushed at the deep compliment. "Stop being charming," I said with a bashful smirk.

My dad cleared his throat, and Kerdik gave him a slight bow. He didn't have to show deference, but chose to all the same. Dad was none too pleased. "You'll show yourself out."

Kerdik touched the yellow roses in the stone vase that he'd grown for me. They'd never wilted in all the time they'd sat there. "Make sure these get moved to your new room. They've got a warding charm on them. It makes you harder for Brìghde to find, if she goes looking."

"You knew she was gunning for me way back then?"

"No, and I still don't know that now. It's a precaution. The flowers will help ward off the Sluagh, as well. Nothing to ruffle your pretty little feathers about."

My dad's eyes widened. "Why would Brìghde have anything to do with Avalon? Why would she be after

Rosie? Why would she even know my daughter's name?" Then the truth dawned on Urien, tightening his features further. "Of all the women in the kingdom you can treat yourself to, my daughter is not on that list. Brìghde will leave Rosie alone, because you'll turn your affections elsewhere."

Kerdik bristled. "What do you know of my affections?"

"I know they're dangerous. I know they nearly tore apart my castle when you last fancied a woman. I know I won't risk my daughter to them. Love means protecting what's yours. If Rosie truly belongs in your heart, then you should protect her to the point of turning away if doing so would lead malady from the doorstep."

Kerdik's fists clenched. It was clear that he saw my father as an equal he had to reason with, instead of someone he could dominate with a snap of his fingers. "Don't tell me what to do, Urien! You had Morgan for years. You have no idea what I go through, being alone as I am. You'll not take away the one woman who doesn't turn her back on me."

I frowned, not liking where this was heading. Lane rarely laid down any type of law with me. I wasn't so sure how much I was liking having birth parents, if this was how things were going to turn. "Guys, can we just cool it for now? Aren't there bigger things going on?"

It was as if I hadn't spoken. "If you love Rosie as you claim you do, then lead Brìghde away from her. You cannot carry on with my daughter anymore. You've indulged yourself enough." My dad turned to me, his nostrils flared. "And Rosie, you've carried on enough, as well. Kerdik isn't a lost puppy in need of guidance. He's a man, and your heart cannot weather the storm he'll bring down upon it."

I covered my face with my hands. "Oh, jeez. This is so out of hand. I'm with Bastien, Dad. Kerdik and I had a small thing, but we're friends now. Everyone needs to keep their noses out of my business, because I'm doing nothing wrong."

"I'm sure Bastien would be thrilled to know Kerdik is sitting on your bed, holding you and kissing you."

I pointed at Urien, calling him out on his BS. "Sarcasm isn't doing you any favors here, Pops. You two are best friends. Fight over something less ridiculous, like normal men."

"You're with Bastien, yet you're wearing another man's ring on your finger! Take that thing off, Rosie. You know this isn't right."

"Don't you dare take off my ring, Rosie," Kerdik warned with too much gravity for a simple piece of jewelry.

"That's it! Get out! Both of you are being obnoxious. I'll wear a pretty ring because my friend gave it to me when I didn't have many friends in Avalon. It's my first piece of real jewelry, and I don't think I should feel guilty about that." I massaged my temples, ignoring Kerdik's triumphant grin. "And Kerdik, if there's something magically funky about this ring, out with it. I mean it. I was thrown into a well over this thing, and accidentally killed a man with it. Tell me what I'm dealing with here."

Kerdik's snark melted into a dark cloud. "I don't have to explain myself to you."

"You do if you want me to keep this thing on my finger."

My dad crossed his arms over his chest and leaned in the doorframe. "Yes, Kerdik. Tell Rosalie all about the gift you've given her."

Kerdik's fists clenched, and the castle started to tremble. I shouted for him to calm down, but if you can believe it, that didn't work. "I don't have to explain myself to mortals!" he raged, his eyes lined with a wildness that made him look like a madman. Then he grabbed onto the front of my flannel and jerked me to him. "Remember that I love you. No matter what you hear about me, I would sacrifice whole kingdoms to keep you by my side."

Then Kerdik kissed me, mashing his lips to mine despite my protest, and right in front of my father. My imitation of a fight was weak, as were my knees at the passion of Kerdik taking what was so clearly partially his. He released me as Urien came barreling toward him, and vanished into thin air before my dad could attack.

The castle stopped trembling, but I could not.

3

A LUXURY STAY AT HOTEL AVALON

After my things were all moved to a frill-less south-facing stone room with no windows, and my dad had exhausted himself with a lecture I only partially listened to, I flopped down on my cot next to my pile of blankets with Walter. My raccoon was the only one with a foul mood to rival mine. "I get it, Dad. Don't kiss a boy just because he's nice to you. Don't take candy from strangers. Don't hop into bed with almighty warlocks. I've had kind of a long day. Could we revisit this another time? I'm sure you've got more important things to do than the whole overprotective parent bit."

Urien stared at me with a hard gaze that tried to peel back the layers I'd built up over the years. They'd come from not having a dad to answer to, but now all of a sudden, here he was. "Kerdik will only bring trouble for you. It's his nature. He doesn't know any different."

"Wow. For his best friend, you don't seem too fond of him. No wonder he clings so hard when he finally finds someone who doesn't write him off."

"I love Kerdik, but that doesn't mean I don't see him as he is. If you had a daughter, and you knew what would happen if she got too close to him, would you allow it? At best, we're talking a broken heart. At worst, my sweet girl mutates into a monster that I'll have no choice but to kill."

"For the last time, I'm not having sex with Kerdik. That was never on the table to begin with. Bastien is my boyfriend."

"Yes, you'll do well to remember that."

"It's what I just said!" I snapped. "Kerdik's my friend."

"Kerdik loves you. He would tear the sun from the sky, ignore Avalon while it withered and died, just so you had something shiny to play with."

"Oh, jeez. Enough with the dramatics." I shook my head at my dad. "This isn't what I want to do with the time we have together. I want to pal around and have fun. I want to talk shop. If I wanted to talk about boyfriend stuff, then I would, and the conversation would be entirely about Bastien, and zero about Kerdik."

Walter murmured about our bickering, and kept up a steady stream of disparaging remarks about me, which I tried to ignore.

Urien looked like he wanted to say something surly, but he put on his kingly airs and refrained. "Very well. Do you have everything you need for the night?"

"I do."

Urien let out a heavy sigh, and I knew part of his frustration wasn't with me. Ruling was rough – especially with such an uncertain territory. This was half the entire kingdom, which was more than he'd ever ruled – and he was doing it alone. "I'll see you in the morning, then. See to it you stay in here, or else you'll be privy to yet another argument about bricking materials and wells, and how there aren't enough of them to satisfy the needs of the new travelers."

My gut twinged, twisting me toward my dad, and away from our fight. Despite our argument, I stood and cleared the distance between us, so I could fling my arms around his neck. "I'm sorry we fought. I love you, and I know you're in a rough spot. You have to worry about so much."

I could feel his cheek lift in a smile against mine as he bent to accommodate my lesser height. "So long as you're safe, that's one worry I can cross off my list. I'm sorry I was cross with you. I worry, is all."

"I know. But I'm grown now. I'm pretty decent at navigating my own pitfalls."

"Yes. I wish with all my heart that I had something to do with that, but I suspect I should thank Lane yet again for her wisdom in raising you."

I kissed his cheek in lieu of a quick cheer-you-up response. I couldn't imagine not being able to raise my own kid, and then trying to figure out how to assert myself once said child was grown. "Go be the best king in all of Avalon."

"I'll do my utmost." Then my dad pulled away, so he could give me a gracious bow before he exited.

The room was about half as large as my bedroom, but it was unfinished, and basically a cavernous stone room with a high ceiling. There was no bed, all my stuff was shoved in a corner. I wasn't sure if it felt like I was changing rooms, or moving into an isolation chamber.

After three days and three nights of the candlelit dank room, I was more than a little stir-crazy. Montel and Link stopped in periodically to make sure I was still alive, but today, I was crawling the walls with the anxiety that comes from being locked in a stone room for your own good. When Link opened the door, I all but attacked him with a ferocious hug. "Please don't lock me in here anymore!" I begged. "It's cold and Walter hates me."

"Jays, you're freezing! Why don't ye wrap up in the blankets we left here?"

"I have been. Tell me you're almost on top of the Sluagh. Tell me this is almost over."

"In a blink, your old Link will have him skewered and filleted over a spit." Link snapped his thick fingers to illustrate his point.

I grimaced. "Gross. Please tell me a joke, or sing me one of your songs or something. Any word from Bastien, Mad and Draper?"

Link's merriment died down. "Not yet. I'm sure they're

alright. Two Untouchables and a prince against an evil queen and her army? No contest. I'd put my money on Mad and Bastien any day."

"Did I ever tell you you're my favorite monkey?"

Link's lopsided grin was in full swing. "Ah, nice try. I see you're trying to charm me into letting ye roam about the castle. No can do, wee Rose."

I harrumphed. "Can I at least have a paper and something to write with? I've been thinking about my dad's problem with the bickering over the wells, and I think I can help."

"Is tha so? I was thinking more along the lines of ye staying in here and keeping your nose outta mischief, but tha doesn't seem possible for ye."

"Paper and quill, Warden," I requested.

"Oh, alright. I guess ye can't get into too much trouble with just tha." Of course, Link locked me inside my dim, dank, windowless room with the grumbling Walter until he came back. "Here. Is tha all? I was thinking of heading out for a few to see if some of the lasses wanted to show their favorite Untouchable some love."

"Have fun, Link."

He kissed my cheek before he left me to my madness.

4

SWEET AND DYSFUNCTIONAL

*M*adness, indeed. I wanted to help my dad and Lane's people. If they were having a hard time getting water to their homes, that was a problem I could maybe help fix. Instead of building a wall, I could take a page from my Ancient Rome history lessons.

I was terrible at drawing, but worse with words, so I did my best to draw from memory the things I'd thought I'd never need to remember beyond taking the exam (that I'd barely passed with a D+). I knew the material; Judah and I had made a 3D map of Ancient Rome, complete with aqueducts and a colosseum we planned on throwing raves in for our little army guys we'd used as civilians in the display. I did my best to create an aerial view drawing, but halfway through, I knew I'd gotten the dimensions wrong.

Quills came with no erasers, so I overthought every

stroke and dip in the ink. I did my best to lay out a map of Avalon as I understood it, with the two wells clearly marked. From there, I drew a series of streets, with the aqueducts lining what I assumed would be cobblestone, once we'd finished it. I'd need Judah for the actual dimensions. Numbers always got confused in my brain, especially ones I hadn't had to remember since high school.

I wanted so badly to help my dad – to save the day in a real way that might take some of the burdens off his shoulders. I wanted to help the people who'd given up the creature comforts in Province 1 to follow us here. I didn't want to be useless, holed up in a dim room because some angry soul-sucker thought the formidable Untouchable had a thing for me. Lame. Mad didn't want me like that. He had a pretty low tolerance for most people. In fact, I was pretty certain if Mad got tested for Autism Spectrum in my world, he'd come back borderline Asperger's.

I wanted my story to be one that made Avalon proud, and that spoke of how Lane raised me to stand with my head high. But my head wasn't high right now. I was frustrated that I couldn't remember the dimensions of an aqueduct, and knew that my map wasn't totally correct. I began to fear the worst: I was a stupid girl, who was only good for one thing. My status was happenstance, and I would never be worthy of all the hype that had gone into my birth and the whole royalty hoopla. Despite my best efforts, if I showed my dad this attempt at a plan, all he would know was that I was stupid, not that I was an asset. I was the girl who was supposed to wear the dresses, and nothing more.

I didn't want to be that girl. I didn't even own any dresses in my real life on earth. Though I'd been steadily at the bottom of the curve of every class ever, I'd never been useless. I was determined Avalon wouldn't change the fundamental parts of me, and tried my very best to help the kingdom from inside these four stone walls.

I willed my tears not to fall to the paper, and like good little soldiers, they obeyed. The bloody tears freaked me out on many levels – the biggest of which was that they obscured my vision. It was like being punished for showing emotion, muting my sight until I calmed the crap down. I tried to breathe through the taunts that, these days, mostly came from myself in my life of seclusion.

Know who you are, Lane's voice echoed in my heart.

I wasn't the girl who sobbed on the floor. Well, I didn't want to be that girl, anyway. I was the girl who showed up day after day, studying all night and persevering through too many cards stacked against her. I was the girl who turned up my middle fingers at the guidance counselors and teachers who tried to veer me away from applying for college. I was the girl who would be a veterinarian someday, taking care of the creatures who couldn't speak for themselves. I was annoyingly persistent when I wanted something, and what I wanted was to help the people who were looking to me for answers.

I didn't know how to be helpful, so I moved away from the parchment and sat in the center of the room, crossing my legs and relaxing my shoulders. I closed my eyes and focused on my slow breathing. Meditation had been more Lane's thing than mine, but if that was my only tool, I wouldn't sneeze at it. I focused on thinking positive thoughts for the people out there, willing tranquility to their hearts, which in turn reminded me to be calm.

When Link came to check on me, I wouldn't open the door for him, though I was desperate for the company. Loneliness gnawed at me, and teamed up with a desperation to get to Judah and Lane, who were no doubt terrified.

"Ye don't want your supper?" Link asked through the door.

"No, thanks. I'm not hungry." It was a bad lie; I was ravenous. But I was more prideful than hungry, and didn't want Link to see me falling apart because I was too dumb to draw a map, and I knew he wouldn't understand meditation. I cursed my uselessness and my inability to draw a map. I could get anywhere, thanks to my inner Compass, but maps were utter gibberish to me, with words and nonsensical abbreviations going upways and slantways and every which way.

I'd thought Link would go away, but he barged in, doing as he pleased, which was no great surprise. "What's wrong?"

I shook my head, my cheeks burning with chagrin as I

crumpled up my poor attempt at a map. "Nothing. Just having a frustrated moment. You can go do your thing."

Link moseyed to the middle of the unadorned stone floor with a look that told me he didn't give a crap about my pride. "Frustrated with this saferoom? I can't imagine how anyone wouldn't revel in this here luxury." He sat on the cot that I'd pushed up to the wall in the corner of the room, and patted the empty space next to him. "Come keep me company."

When I could tell he wasn't going anywhere, I exhaled out the last of my self-loathing and frustration, and plopped down next to him. I breathed easier as I sunk into his outstretched arm. "How's dad? Any updates on the kingdom? Any word from the search party?"

"No word from them. The kingdom's restless without Lane, but tha's to be expected. Seeing ye so often out at the wall gave them all some assurance that everything was alright. Now tha you're not there, people are getting scared."

"If I haven't said anything before, I hate this plan."

"Ye might've mentioned tha a time or two before." He squeezed my bicep as he leaned against the cold stone wall. "Ye know ye have to stay hidden. Kerdik's trying to draw the Sluagh away. It's for the good of your kingdom tha you're in here. If the Sluagh gets hungry, he could start sucking the souls out of your people."

I stretched my arm around his stomach, letting myself

relax in his half-embrace. "I know, I just feel useless, is all. I should be helping them build the wall. Dad shouldn't have to hold court alone. You're making sure there's enough security for him when he meets with the people?"

"Aye." Link kissed my forehead. "Ye worry about everyone. It makes ye a good ruler, but it'll turn your insides miserable after a while. Just be here with me for a minute before ye go rattling off all the things tha need fixing."

"You're right. Sorry." I forced myself to take a deep breath and exhale out enough of my worries so that I was able to enjoy the simple gift of loving contact when I'd been isolated for so long. "You stink like sex," I commented with my nose wrinkled.

"I'll take tha as a compliment."

"Depends on if the girl looks half as satisfied and cocky as you do right now."

Link sniggered. "Aye. She was plenty pleased with me. And I was plenty pleased with her." His eyebrows did a suggestive little dance "Twice."

"You ever think about settling down with anyone?" I asked, lightly tickling his side.

"Nah. It's too much fun to have new bounty thrown at me daily. One woman when I can have them all? I don't see the draw. Bastien got himself all twisted up for ye, and I don't see it having done him no favors."

I sat up straighter. "Hey!"

"Not that ye aren't worth the daily risk of putting his

life in danger, traveling across a country just to make sure ye have a bit of family to come home to. It's just not for me."

"You're a romantic, if I haven't told you before. Feed lines like that to the ladies, and they'll eat it up. 'Baby, I wouldn't cross an ocean for you, but I'd probably like, walk a block or so.'"

Link blew out a raspberry. "I don't need a line. I'm Untouchable. My tattoo says enough."

"You're super charming," I said with too much saccharine dripping from my sarcasm.

"Besides, now that we have ye in the group, there's no need to settle down. If I want a roll in the hay, I go find a willing lass. If I want a snuggle and a talk, I have ye. Best of both worlds."

"I'm your rent-a-wife? That had better come with perks."

"Aye, it does. Once Avalon is settled, ye won't have to lift a finger again in your life. You'll have the Brotherhood to do the lifting for ye."

"Oh, how well you know me," I simpered. A life with nothing to do sounded horrible. "I wonder if Avalon ever will get settled, and what that would look like. Do you think Faîte will ever get its mojo back?" I wondered idly. "Bastien told me once that Avalon used to have more magic than this – that it wasn't all so dependent on the Jewels of Good Fortune."

"Tha was before my time." Link's arm stayed securely

around me, his thumb brushing up and down my side lazily. I guess I really was becoming his rent-a-wife. "Everyone thinks more magic, more power, will solve all the problems, but it won't. It'll just mean more policing of the new problems tha'll come. If the people can't work together when they have nothing, then they can't be trusted with everything."

"Careful, otherwise I'll start thinking you're wise, and not just pretty." My eyebrows furrowed together. "What sort of problems? I thought more magic is what everyone wanted. The good old days, and all that. The Jewels of Good Fortune being in the area has been great for the land, except for all the warfare."

"Your country hasn't seen Vampires or Werewolves like Éireland has. To Avalon, I'm sure having the higher magic back would be a return to the good old days – until the fighting for more power and resources starts up again."

"Vampires and Werewolves? Yikes. We've got stories about those in Common. Just pretend stories, of course. Lots of times they're spun into romances."

Link crinkled his nose and looked at me to see if I was joking. "No, *Vampires* and *Werewolves*," he repeated, as if I'd heard him incorrectly.

"I know what those are."

"Common must be some twisted place, if they're weaving tales of romance out of rabid blood-sucking creatures and Werebeasts." He shook his head, tightening his arm around me, as if he expected the extinct creatures to come roaring through the door at any moment. "Tha the foul creatures might come back?" He shuddered. "If ye think your Da has his hands full now, you've no idea the mess he'll have to stay on top of if the Vamps tha used to live in Éireland come into his territory. I'd gladly move up to Common and forfeit all my magic just to be rid of tha nightmare." He paused to laugh, but the sound was bitter and laced with disbelief. "I can't imagine a book where a Werewolf or a Vampire's the lead in a love story. How would tha even work? They don't slow down to get all gooey before they pounce; they just attack, and ye don't get back up."

"Do they obey the code of the Untouchables?"

"They can't think to reason it out tha far. The Vamps only see blood, and the Weres only see meat. No, no. Higher magic back in Avalon would be a disaster. Sure, ye might be able to fly or heal people easier. Ye could renew nature without the jewels, but the price tag isn't worth the trade. We've got enough problems with regular attacks without adding those beasts into the mix." His thick fingers squeezed my shoulder, and then reached down to flip my wrist over to get a look at my tattoo. He pressed his wrist to the side of mine, letting the visual of the team spirit sink in. "Our mark looks good on ye."

I leaned my head against his cheek, grateful he was here. Grateful for so many things, really. "If I never said so before, thanks for convincing me to get the Untouchables tattoo. I like being part of your family. I love you guys."

He kissed my temple, his full lips leaving a trace of wetness on my skin. I didn't wipe it away; I loved him too much not to keep every bit of him – slobber and all. "Even though your situation's turning out to be a bigger job than we'd planned, I wouldn't have us without ye in the mix." He sighed heavily. "We cling to those of us in the Brotherhood. We're all we have." The corner of his mouth lifted with his natural caddish charm to cover over the melancholy. "I'm glad we have ye now."

My fingers trailed up his torso to rub the ache in his chest that he wouldn't admit to aloud. For several contented minutes, Link and I snuggled on the cot holding each other – two rootless misfits trying to make the best of a world gone wrong. "Did anyone explain to Annabelle that I can't have a tea party with her because I'm holed up in here?"

"Aye. Only we told her ye had work in the province, not tha you're still in the palace. Annabelle's with Aimee and Faith. They've been having a ball, dressing her up in all sorts of fancy gowns. They've been instructed to keep her with them on the first floor, so she's safe. I told her ye were going out into the province to buy her sweets." He turned pensive for a moment. "Little thing lit up like a lantern. Said she'd never had a sweet before."

I waited a few beats while I sat, tucked into Link's side, mulling over his words. "That's a sad song, old man."

"Aye, but it's the only one tha makes sense in this

world. Why do ye think I was so keen on ye getting our mark? Too many sad songs to go around."

I craned my head to look up at him. "I'm still not sure why you wanted me to get the mark so badly. You knew Bastien wasn't totally committed back then."

"Sure, but I knew he'd get his head on right in the end, and he did, true enough. No one's more loyal to ye now than he is. But I pushed so hard because I took a shine to ye, and so did Mad. Mad doesn't... He's not the cuddly type. When he opens up and talks to a woman, I take note. I have a lot less to worry about, now tha you've got our mark. Sure, Bastien has ye, but now Mad and I do, as well."

"I can't decide if that's sweet, or totally dysfunctional."

"Can't it be both? I'm usually both."

I sniggered and let him move my tattooed hand to rest on his chest, savoring the comforting touch while I had it. Three days with very little contact had been rough, to say the least. "Do you think Bastien's alright?"

"Aye. I think now tha he knows he belongs to ye, nothing will hold him back from giving ye everything ye need, and coming home to us in one piece. He's at his best when he's rife with purpose. Falls apart a little without it."

When the door's handle rattled, I made to open it, but Link held his arm in front of me to keep me back. He shook his head at me in warning. "Your Da's holding court, and he has a key to this room. So does Montel. Those are the only people who know you're in here. The staff even thinks you're gone," he whispered. Slowly, Link lowered his hand to his belt and slid out his short sword, doing his best to mute the metallic sound. It was freeing itself to do his bidding, readying to serve the Brotherhood. A gravelly whisper sounded from the other side of the solid door, and Link practically knocked me over with his emphatic gestures that the Sluagh was finally here for me.

5

TRAPPED AND PECKED

I'd gone from snuggly puppy time with Link, to clutching my fists on high alert as he angled his body in front of mine. He moved to the wall and felt around for a groove I'd hoped we wouldn't have to use. My teeth were set on edge when a tiny door swung out from the wall. I peered inside the crawlspace this room had been chosen for, due to the flawless stone camouflage. "In," Link mouthed, with no room for argument.

"I don't want to leave you to fight by yourself!" I pleaded, afraid for him.

Link managed a quick smile for me and smooched my lips. "Stay in there until I come get ye. Quiet, now."

I obeyed, but only because I was unarmed, and wasn't sure I'd be much help in a battle with a spirit-like magical being. I didn't know if the traditional fighting methods would even work on the vengeful dude. I grabbed the grousing Walter and crawled into the tight space. I hugged my knees to my chest as Link shut me inside. There was about a foot of breathing room on all four sides, and a foot of space above my head, but it still felt claustrophobic. I closed my eyes, so the pitch black would be my choice.

The shouts and the clanging of swords came not five seconds later, and it took everything inside of me to sit in my prison and not join Link in the fray. My heart pounded with the desire to defend my territory. I don't know when it happened, but somewhere along the lines, the Untouchables had become mine, every bit as much as I'd become theirs. Every nick on Link cut me, as well. I didn't want his body to get further broken down. I couldn't handle yet more scars littering his skin. I shoved my fist in my mouth to keep myself from crying out when I heard him howl. He'd done enough fighting in his life; that phase was supposed to be over.

There was a screeching sound that I hoped meant the good guys had finally won an inch. When Montel's voice joined the fight, I was conflicted between feeling elated that we were outnumbering the enemy, and wanting Montel to run away from the danger. He was only here because of me. If I hadn't needed babysitting, he'd be out on the wall with his dad.

Montel's cries were louder than Link's, and a bit more scared. Though he was usually unruffled and plenty strong, this was an undead spirit monster. I had an unquenchable desire to somehow will Andre the Giant's spirit into the room, for surely if my unstoppable Andre was there, Montel and Link would be safe.

"Where?" the Sluagh breathed. When he spoke, I heard the sound of wings flapping, as if they were coming out of his mouth. There was a cry, a popping sound, and then a slurping noise that made my skin crawl. I knew the satisfied noise from the monster could only mean bad things. The Sluagh seemed to grow agitated. "Where?!"

"Well, your friend's going to die," Walter guessed without much preference either way.

"Mad's not here," Link bellowed, his sword lending itself to another crash. There was a thud, and then the quietness of a flutter of wings. My heart nearly stopped until I heard Link groan, and a stirring near the door I hoped was Montel. "Your fight's with me! I'm the one who murdered the soldiers in the commune!" Link cried, his voice panicking.

Out of nowhere, something gold slipped under the crack of the hidden door and slammed into my chest, knocking me back with a squeak. It was my *lueur*, hot and sizzling in my ribcage. My hands panicked and patted my torso, trying to reason out how I could have my *lueur* back if it was tucked safely inside of Montel.

"Ah. I suspected that might work," the sinister voice of the Sluagh said.

The desperation in Link's voice scared me. "No! Don't go in there! It's me ye want!"

When the crawlspace door banged open, I shrieked as

a large bird-like claw barged in and raked at my arm. Walter slipped out and bolted, not bothering to offer up even a swipe of his paw to help a girl out.

I fought frantically in the tiny space, scrambling to get away until an unkindness of ravens flooded my tiny hideaway. Birds with rotting beaks pecked at my skin, peppering me with scratches and scrapes from head to toe, while I screamed and thrashed. I covered my eyes, but every other spot on my body was fair game for being stabbed with their beaks that felt filed to a point; they were so sharp. Blood bloomed on my arms, and my clothes now had tiny holes all over to show off the small slashes they blessed me with. "Stop!" I tried to command them, but it was clear these were no ordinary birds, but an extension of the monster they served.

When the claw-like hand reached for me again, the Sluagh was able to pull me out with less resistance. His grip exposed me on my hands and knees as he jerked me out into the room. The ravens flew around the windowless room, circling like a black cyclone that waited to suck me up into the ceiling. I looked up and gasped at the haggard and thin bird-like features of the man in the black hooded cloak. He stood only three steps away now, taking his time to get a good look at my fear. His skin was barely hanging onto the bone, and looked leprous in some spots. He had greasy coal-colored stringy hair hanging in his face, and teeth that were chipped and yellow with rot. When his hood fell back, I screamed with all the terror of a woman facing her serial killer in a horror flick.

"A pure soul," he said, and again his words had the sound of flapping wings to them when they birthed from his pointed beak-like dry and cracked lips. His breath stank of rotting fish, churning up the desire to barf all over him. "Madigan's bride will do nicely."

Link was bleeding from his shoulder as he struggled in vain to stand from the stone floor. Montel was eerily motionless in the doorway. The Sluagh chuckled, seeming to draw pleasure from my fear. I didn't know how to fight against the magical spirit-snatcher, but I knew I'd either live or die trying to figure it out. I scrambled to my feet and grabbed Link's abandoned sword that had fallen out of his reach. "Run, Rosie!" he bellowed. I could tell he was in a lot of pain by the pinched sound of his voice.

I don't know why or how, but a sudden calmness swept over me. If I would die in punishment for Madigan avenging himself and cleansing his country, then so be it. Those horrible soldiers turned a sweet boy into an unfeeling soldier. Madigan the Formidable was under my protection, as was Link the Terrifying. If something was after them, I would take up the nearest sword and make my allegiances perfectly clear.

I inhaled slowly when I recalled that this was not the Sluagh's adventure. He'd had his time in the sun. This was *my* adventure, and I wasn't about to let him run the show.

I raised my chin as the Sluagh watched my rolled-back

shoulders and cool deportment with curiosity. "Link, I want you to take Montel and get my father out of the castle. Go now."

"I'll not leave ye here, Rosie! Go! I'll finish him!"

The Sluagh's cloak fell away, and it was then I realized it had never been a cloak covering him, only leathery batwings that had clothed him like a garment this entire time. His gaunt, naked body showed all of his ribs, his skin barely clinging to his pelvic bowl. Though he looked like a distorted corpse, I saw his agility was fully intact. He didn't need muscles like we did. He had a red orb in his chest that glowed like an enlarged heart. E.T. phone home, for sure. It pumped slowly, and each beat shook the organ with such force, I could practically hear it thumping. The red swirled with a gray smoke, and in the smoke, I saw dozens of small eyeballs sweeping across the heart's equator, begging me with fear and pain to end it all for them.

I would not join them in there. I resolved myself that my eyes would stay perfectly intact. My food made a similar pact with my stomach, vowing I would not throw up at the ghastly sight.

"Rosie, go!"

I didn't look away from the Sluagh, but made sure it knew the fight was with me. "He attacked the Brotherhood, Link. I can't walk away from that." Not that the monster would let me stroll out of here, but that was beside the point. I was resolved to make it *my choice* to stay and fight, instead of something that was being forced upon me. I kept that locked tight in my mind as I held my ground, letting it fuel me away from fear and desperation, and bring me toward a warrior's peace. The Brotherhood didn't run from fights; they met them head-on. If these were my people now, then this would be my battle. Link was mine, and I would protect him by whatever means necessary.

6

ONCE UPON A MIDNIGHT DREARY

I gripped the sword, but held it down at my side, a toy in the hands of a kid – not a warrior. The red heart of my enemy drummed out a rhythm that was slow and measured, jerking my focus to the forefront. It zinged me to the part of my brain that stored rap songs and poetry assignments. I ignored Link's pleas for me to run and took a step to the left, leading the focus away from my bleeding friend.

My voice came out quiet as I tapped into my crazy side, using good old schoolwork to ground me, like the studious girl I was. "'Once upon a midnight dreary, while I pondered, weak and weary.'" The words came out of me like a mantra, steadying the sword in my hand. "'Over many a quaint and curious volume of forgotten lore, while I nodded, nearly napping, suddenly there came a tapping.'"

"Your spells won't work on me, child," the Sluagh warned with mild amusement to him.

I didn't care that he wanted to toy with me, to scare me a little by showing me his bird minions and uncloaking before the kill. It was clear he liked the showmanship of his grand evilness, so I refused to give him the fear he craved. Instead I met his intimidation tactics with my very best crazy, reciting poetry even as he tried to scare the "me" out of me. He didn't count on me not freaking out, and using a little of my own madness to toy with him. Slowly, my neck started moving backward and forward, as it always did when I rapped to my heart's content. The rhythm stayed slow to match the red pulse of my enemy; there was no need to hurry the rage that boiled in me when a threat came after someone I loved. Link was under *my* protection now, and that was no small thing. "As of someone gently rapping, rapping at my chamber door. 'Tis some visitor,' I muttered, 'tapping at my chamber door – only this, and nothing more.'"

The Sluagh shrieked at my slam, and his ravens squawked angrily above him. "I'm no visitor. I'm the torture that's going to keep you from the mercy of death."

"'Be that word our sign in parting, bird or fiend,' I shrieked, upstarting. 'Get thee back into the tempest and the Night's Plutonian shore!'" I skipped ahead, hoping old Poe wouldn't mind, my hips joining with a slow sway that gave me the edge of madness my enemy hadn't expected me to possess. I ignored Link's cries for me to run. Maybe I didn't know what I was doing, but I knew who I was. I wouldn't cower. If Morgan hadn't broken me, then this jaggoff didn't have a prayer. I said a silent thanks to my birth mother for taking me so near the edge of my own ending. It gave me confidence, knowing that if I'd survived her evil, then I could stand against anything.

The ravens swirled above me, waiting on word from their master. I knew by the pissed-off look in his bulbous eyes that he'd want to finish me himself. His pride wouldn't let his minions take the credit. The crazy ones got the fun deaths, and I looked about as bonkers as they come. He was perplexed at first at my slow rapping, but that quickly gave way to indignation that I'd stopped cowering. "I'll make sure to leave your friend alive, so he can tell Madigan of the screams ye made when I suck the soul from ye!"

I didn't miss a beat, circling him as if I held the power, which I knew wasn't true. "'Leave no black plume as a token of that lie thy soul hath spoken! Leave my loneliness unbroken! Quit the bust above my door!'" I lifted my sword, but the Sluagh was too confused by my rapping to perceive the threat I would always be when told to cower. "'Take thy beak from out my heart, and take thy form from off my door!'"

"Enough of your spells!" the Sluagh raged, taking a step forward to end my taunting. He took a swipe at me with his claws, but I dodged, offering him an evil smile instead of relief that I'd escaped his advance.

I chuckled like a true sociopath, which maybe by this point, I was. Part of me was looking forward to gutting this dude. I knew that any time someone I loved was threatened, the inner psychotic in me would rise up to defend what was mine. Link was mine, and I was ready to let my inner Morgan fly free, mangling a life to save my kingdom.

Another claw shot out at me, raking my arm and drawing blood. The deep grooves bloomed quickly with crimson, but instead of gasping, I only laughed, as if I'd wanted him to do that all along. Maybe part of me did. Now that he'd punished me for Madigan's sins, I felt absolved as my fist gripped the sword with a purpose I couldn't back down from. I took a chance and asked my Compass where to deliver a lethal hit. My gut practically leapt out of my body to pierce itself through the manky dude's glowing heart. My wicked grin couldn't be tamed.

I'd learned through the years that *I* couldn't be tamed, either.

The Sluagh let out a screech of fury at my laughter.

My focus lasered in on the anger radiating from him, which was now partially mixed with fear. I exhaled with a smile, knowing, as any decent soccer player knew, that if you psych out the other team, the game is in the bag.

The ravens descended as I plunged the sword into the Sluagh's red pulsing heart, stabbing through the eyes of the souls he'd trapped. I let out a scream of vengeance that scared even me. I didn't know if this was the way to go, but seeing those eyes begging to be freed of their limbo seemed like something to cross off the to-do list.

The second the sword pierced the pulsing heart, a sonic boom echoed across the room and belted out through the castle, rattling windows and shaking the ground.

Link cried out in shock, and I heard footsteps of the household staff coming to our rescue far too late. I pushed the sword in deeper, shrieking at the ravens who pierced me all over. Their rotting beaks looked like yellowed Swiss cheese, but I felt nothing except a spiteful victory that I'd landed a lethal hit on someone who'd come after the Brotherhood.

Satisfied though I was with the solid hit, I didn't stop. I pushed the sword in until the hilt slammed against the Sluagh's brittle ribs, my nose an inch from his. His sour breath bathed my face as he cried out in anguish and surprise, no doubt shocked that little old me had used my crazy to take down the evil spirit monger. I leaned in just to satisfy my own sadism, and finished the poem with a low and breathy, "'Quoth the Raven, 'Nevermore.'"

7

NEVER MORE. NEVER AGAIN.

"Never again. And I mean, never, ever again will I witness what I saw tonight. You were supposed to be in the saferoom!" Urien was pissed, but I was too worked up to put on a good show of being contrite.

"That's exactly where I was. It's not my fault that the bad guy yanked me out of the hidey-hole and tried to kill me. Did you want me to just stand there and let him finish me off?"

My dad had gone from yelling, to squashing me in a hug, to releasing me so Jean-Luc could treat my millions of tiny cuts. Then he repeated the pattern over and over. He didn't allow me more than a foot of space. I'd been allowed to leave the saferoom, and was grateful to be reunited to my bedroom again. It had windows, which was a sizable step up from my previous lodging situation.

Dad's mouth was set in a tight line, and he talked with his hands, just like I did when I got too worked up. He was kind of precious. "You weren't supposed to have to fight. That's the whole point of having security assigned specifically to you."

I lowered my chin, lest it tremble and give away that I was on the verge of a breakdown. I breathed steadily through my nose, keeping my voice level and low. "I'll tell Pascal what happened."

"Not a chance. You're lying down just as soon as Jean-Luc finishes up. Link and I can tell Pascal what happened to his son." Then my dad turned to my healer. "Has she lost much blood?"

Jean-Luc looked at my dad as if to say, *"What do you think?"*

"I'm fine. Just freaking out a little, is all. That dude was janky."

"Indeed. You pierced him through in the one place you could've killed him. That's some luck you've got. It seems to keep you barely alive, and perpetually wounded. Though I guess I can't complain, as you survived. You could've had your soul sucked into his heart, you know, just like Montel."

I nodded, knowing I couldn't sidestep that warning. "He really sucked out Montel's soul?"

Link nodded from my bed. "Aye. There was no stopping him. Ye did Montel a kindness, murdering the

Sluagh. Now Montel's soul can rest. He only had a brief stop in limbo before ye freed him."

"You mean before I let him get murdered. I didn't free Montel. He died because he was watching out for me." My gaze cut to my dad. "You're sure nothing wonky happened to my *lueur*? It just went back into me, no muss, no fuss?"

"That's how it works, yes. If your *Guardien* passes, the *lueur* is returned to its owner, good as new."

I waved off Jean-Luc's efforts to bandage every cut I'd received. The larger, more problematic ones had been taken care of well enough. "Montel was good to me. He was my friend. He walked me home after work every night just because Draper asked him to. He took my *lueur*," my chin quivered, and I wished everyone would just get the crap out of my room. "I got Montel killed."

"He died protecting the throne. There's no higher honor," my dad ruled.

"Who cares about honor when you're dead?"

Link's shoulder had been stitched and bandaged, along with the deep slice on his calf I hadn't noticed in the chaos. "His Da will care about honor, and when there's no more life to have, we cling to the only thing left. Urien will gift Pascal with a medal tha hangs over the doorway to his home, letting everyone know tha Pascal raised a warrior. He'll be respected in the village for it."

My dad hugged me, and after much reassurance that I was fine (I mean, honestly, I had dozens of glorified papercuts, and Link had actually severed something that sounded important. I was fine), he and Jean-Luc left us to the quiet of my room.

I stood by the window, peering out at the world I couldn't touch until I'd healed up enough that the people didn't freak out at the sight of me. Dad explained that I was their touchstone, so a cut on me was read as a danger aiming at them. If *I* couldn't escape unscathed, then they would lose hope that they were living in a safe place.

A bird landed on the sill, squawking at me to open up and let him inside. I wanted to let him in, but knew I couldn't. I'd tried to open the windows before, but the magic Kerdik had sealed me inside with kept me from even cracking a window to let in a little fresh air.

"How'd ye know to stab the Sluagh there? Did Kerdik tell ye?"

I shook my head, my eyes still on the bird I couldn't quite hear. I leaned in and pressed my palm to the window, wanting to stroke the feathers that ruffled in the slight breeze. I'd let Walter go free, and he couldn't get away from me fast enough. I longed to be near an animal who wanted my company. "I saw the eyeballs swirling around in the heart thing he had, and my Compass told me that was where to land the kill hit. I guessed, is all."

"Tha sure was lucky. I tried to get to ye, but he stuck my leg worse than I was expecting. Nasty bugger. I'm sorry I failed ye, Rosie."

I glanced at him over my shoulder and quirked my eyebrow. "You didn't fail me. You tried to save me. It was just my turn to save you this time, is all."

"Aye, and ye did tha beautifully." He was quiet a few beats. "What was tha spell ye were casting? I didn't think ye had witchery magic, other than your birth blessings."

I snorted, my eyes on the bird who stared at me with longing. "I don't. It wasn't magic at all. It was pieces of a poem. I think I snapped or something. It calmed me down when I was on the verge of losing my shiz. I don't like when the people I love get snatched at."

Link rubbed his chest and smiled at me, letting me know I belonged to him. I was covered in cuts, and a little disheveled, yet I was precious to someone wonderful. "I love ye, too, wee Rose. But the next time I tell ye to run, do as I say."

"And not as you do? Like you would've run away if I couldn't defend myself," I scoffed. "Don't tell me to be less like you. I can't imagine anything more terrible."

"*Much* less," he pressed, his eyes suddenly serious. "Don't ye understand what ye mean to Bastien? If he'd come home and ye weren't there to greet him? I'd be sending myself off to the Forgotten Forest with my shame, letting his life implode like tha."

"Hello, I'm not Bastien's whole life. You're being dramatic. And don't you even think about going to the Forgotten Forest. Not for a single second. Avalon without your smile? We'd have to rely on simple sunshine to brighten the world, and that's just plain not enough."

Link blinked twice at my compliment, and touched his finger to his heart to let me know that one had stuck in there deep.

I turned back to the window, frustrated that I couldn't hear the bird, who was chirping his heart out. Out of sheer frustration, I gave the pane a push, shocked when it actually popped open. "What the..." Kerdik had seen to it that I was sealed inside. I wasn't supposed to be able to open any of the doors or windows.

The bird flew in and landed on my finger, singing me a song to tell me that his flock had snubbed any ravens that might happen to pass by. Link hadn't put together that me opening a window was a big deal. Everyone else had been able to come and go as they pleased, but whenever I'd tried to open a door, or sneak through when someone else left it open, I couldn't inch a single toe into freedom.

Now I had options.

I petted my new friend with two fingers. "No, no. I don't want you to be mean. The nasty ravens are all gone now. Being a raven doesn't make you bad, just that one flock, and they're gone now. So you don't have to treat all ravens like they might hurt me. They won't. I want you to be nice, alright? Can you spread that around?"

The bird flitted onto my shoulder while I surreptitiously moved around the room and quietly started stuffing clothes and provisions into a knapsack. "This room is a mess," I explained when Link quirked his eyebrow at me. Hopefully it just looked like I was cleaning. When I had enough shoved into the pack, I made sure my voice was light and airy. "I'm hungry. You want me to grab you something from the kitchen?"

"Sure. Whatever you're having, triple it, and tha's what I'll eat."

I let out a nervous chuckle at the subterfuge that was finally within my grasp. I could escape. I could be useful. I could run. "Cool." I slid on my shoes and slipped out of the room. I quickly tiptoed down the stone steps, hoping the staff didn't greet me too loudly when I inevitably ran into them along the way. I gave sweet Mercy a cheery smile when I reached the kitchen.

"Oh, Princess! So many cuts. Are you alright?"

"Better than ever." I worked up a grin, wishing she wasn't so near to tears at the sight of my cuts. My dad was right; the people saw themselves when they saw me. If I'd escaped Morgan le Fae, then they could leave, as well. If I had slices on my skin from a monster, then they felt attacked, too.

I shoved a few rolls, and some peaches from the bowl on the counter into my pack when she had her back turned so she could sniffle into her handkerchief. It wasn't enough food, but I didn't have many options if I wanted to cut and run before anyone else intercepted me.

When my pack was ganked from my hands, I whirled around to face the thief. Link grinned down at me with a knowing smile that told me I wasn't as sneaky as I'd hoped. "Well, what do we have here? Did ye get me a wee present?" He tugged out a tank top of mine and eyed it appreciatively. "I'm not sure it'll fit me, but I'll give it a go." He shoved my shirt over his head, looking like the Hulk trying on a doll's outfit. He finally gave up getting his arms through the holes, and wore it around his neck like a choker. "Fits perfect. Cheers, Rosie. Ye always get me the best gifts. Let's go upstairs, and I'll tell you all the ways I'm extra grateful ye are so very predictable."

His meaty hand gripped my bicep, informing me that I had no choice in the matter, and that he was miffed at me for trying to give him the slip. "Oh, fine."

Link practically dragged me up the steps, waiting until the door was shut behind us to yell at me. "Are ye out of your mind? Where did ye think ye were scampering off to?"

I shrugged. "I was going to see if I could help out with Bastien and them."

"I swear, if ye weren't already so daft, I'd knock ye in the head. You're the same mule as Bastien. Ye deserve each other. Master Kerdik put ye in this house, and your Da said for ye to stay here, so tha's where you'll be." He moved to the opened window. "Did ye really think I'd miss tha? I don't know how Master Kerdik's magic went sour, but it's no matter. I don't need magic to keep ye in place." He slapped his massive bicep. "I've got these. Try your tricks, lass. I've seen it all."

"Morgan doesn't want them," I argued. "She wants me. She wants my ring. She can have it, for all I care. If I can help get Lane and them all back, shouldn't I? Judah's my best friend, Link. You don't know Judah. He can't handle Avalon! Morgan's got him locked up, Link! Judah's delicate!"

"Delicate?" Link scrunched his nose. "I can't imagine ye with a bloke who's delicate."

"Let's go together," I suggested. "I wouldn't be out of your sight. We could ride out right now and track them down."

"You're batty," he observed, stepping back and pressing his spine to the closed door. He was a wall of muscle, and I knew there was no way I could get by him.

I ran my hands through my hair, frustrated and growing desperate. I didn't know how long my window of freedom might last. "You don't understand, because you're cool!"

"I'm cool?" he repeated, amused. "I understand well enough the fear that comes with losing the one person ye can count on. When I lost Mad?" He shook his head with sadness. "I understand better than ye think."

"You've got friends everywhere you look. You walk into a room, and women throw themselves at you. Men want to be you. I didn't have that. Lane camouflaged my body so Morgan's spies wouldn't be able to find me. I had a hump and acne. I had a lazy eye and a learning disability. No one was throwing themselves at me. No one wanted to be my friend, except for Lane and Judah. Judah didn't care what I looked like; he only cared that we were best friends. You have no idea how rare it is to find someone who loves you unconditionally, because *everyone* loves you! You weren't Remedial Rosie. You weren't the Humpback Whale. You weren't the only one not invited to every single birthday party in the second grade. You don't know what it feels like to have someone stand with you when no one else will. Judah's my Brotherhood. Judah's my family, and right now, he's caught up in Avalon's drama because my mom hates me that much! She hates me so much that she'd take my Lane and my Judah, all to try and get at my jewelry." I thumbed my ring. "She can have it, for all I care! I want my family back!"

Link scooped me up in a one-armed hug to quiet my hysterics. "Okay, okay. Settle, now. Bastien knows how much ye need your mammy and your brother. He won't come home without them. Trust him to get the job done."

"Judah's not built for this kind of world." I gripped his t-shirt, feeling the hard muscles beneath. "He's the reason I know that poem I used to distract the Sluagh. He taught it to me. It's because of him I'm alive right now, and didn't get the soul sucked out of me. Even before Avalon, I was so miserable, Link. Kids can be cruel, but Judah made up for all of that. He always stuck up for me, and you're asking me to leave him with Morgan?"

"I'm not asking ye anything. I'm telling ye tha there's no way I'm letting ye anywhere near your crazy mammy.

Never again." He clumsily patted my back. "Ye really had a hump and all tha? I wondered how the Commoner men could be so daft as to let ye slip through their fingers. It makes a little more sense with tha filter. Shortsighted fools."

"Link, you have to..." I was working out my next plea, but suddenly the room vanished from my vision. A white light flooded my view, pushing out the details of my bedroom. "Link? Link!" I gripped him, scared that I'd suddenly somehow gone blind. I could feel his musculature, but I couldn't see a thing.

"Rosie? What's wrong? What's happening to your eyes? The pink one's turning red! Rosie, stop it!"

I clawed at him, afraid of the brightness I couldn't escape. Then suddenly, a face materialized before me. I didn't recognize the flaming red hair, the high cheekbones, the sunken-in cheeks or the bright blue eyes. I didn't recognize the woman with the mannish hands, dressed in a moss-colored gown with a crown of twisted vines atop her curls. She yelled at me in my vision, and I jumped in Link's arms. "Ye think ye can come here after all this time and ask me for favors?" Her overlarge nostrils flared with temper as she glared at me. "Understand this, my green friend: the only thing tha would make me happier is if there was a cure to our immortality. I would gladly end you, if there was tha possibility. As it is, ending everyone you love is a grand second choice."

I gripped Link's face, but couldn't see him. I only saw

the woman with hate burning in her eyes. Words came out of my mouth that didn't belong to me. When I spoke, I heard Kerdik's voice instead. "How droll to use up your attentions on me. You always were obsessed. How very small your kingdom must be, to afford you all this free time. Remember well our night between the sheets, do you? Was I so good that after decades, you still burn for me? Tell me, Brìghde, did you go after Tara out of hatred for me, or jealousy because I chose a mere handmaiden over you?"

Brìghde's nostrils flared again. When she raised her hands, foot-long thorns shot out of her palms, piercing Kerdik all over. I felt his pulse quicken, but didn't experience his pain. "I know your patterns. I know your desires. You'll choose a virgin to defile when ye get so lonely tha ye risk mating again. She'll be meek, and think the world rises and falls on your shoulders. She'll pretend she doesn't mind your green hands on her body, but she'll shiver in disgust, Kerdik. Mark my words, old friend, it was only me who ever fancied ye, and ye betrayed me."

Kerdik's voice came out of my mouth again, and I felt Link lowering my body to the wooden floor of my bedroom, while I trembled through the scene I had no right to be witnessing. "I wouldn't have bothered if I'd known you had so little going on in your life. One betrayal shouldn't equal unending vengeance. Have you truly found no one who can satisfy you after all these years? Do mortals pale in comparison to how well I pleased you so long ago? It's the only explanation."

Brighde screamed her fury at Kerdik, but didn't strike out this time. "Don't make a joke of my affections. I loved ye, and ye used me! I left my husband for ye, and then ye were gone!"

8

BRÌGHDE, KERDIK'S EX

Kerdik took a chance and stepped forward. I felt my foot moving in time with his, though since I was laying on the floor, I didn't go anywhere. He leaned in and spoke low in her ear. "It was you who used me, if I remember correctly. Over and over again, you took everything I gave you. How sad you haven't been pleased since then." He shrugged and stepped back. "That's the difference between mortals and us, I guess."

Brìghde wound up and slapped him across the face, snapping my head and his to the side. I could hear Link calling my name and patting my cheek, but it all took a backseat to the scene I was living out through Kerdik. "Tell me you're miserable because of me," Brìghde seethed. "Tell me you've found the love of your eternal lives, but ye can't have her because of me." She must've seen something in Kerdik's eyes, because she chuckled darkly. "Oh, grand. I haven't seen a dragon in so very long. Tell me, who is the poor lass who had the rotten luck to draw your eye?"

"There's no one."

"You lie. Poorly, too. You used to be so much better at deception."

"She's protected, so there's nothing you can do to touch her. And thanks to you, there's nothing *I* can do to touch her, either. I'm tortured even without your help, because she doesn't want me in the ways she should."

Brìghde let out a gratified, throaty laugh. "Oh, tha is far better than my curse. What magic does she carry tha even I can't tear out her heart through her chest to wrap it up as a present for ye?"

Kerdik's voice was steady. "I gave her Faîte's lost magic. She doesn't know it, of course, but it's been with her for a while now."

My horrified intake of breath was the only reaction I was permitted as the scene continued to unfold.

Brìghde scoffed. "Faîte's magic? Ye wouldn't dare unleash tha. Nor would ye trust it with a mortal. It took the three of us too long to bottle up."

Kerdik didn't bother arguing. "I came here to warn you not to touch Rosie. Word will reach your lands soon enough that the Avalon Rose caught my eye."

"The Avalon Rose? The Lost Princess? The one ye gave the birth blessings to?"

Kerdik's voice was dripping with disdain at having to

have this chat and reveal so many of his cards. "Do you know of any other Avalon Roses?"

"Tha was a cruel blessing. I remember trying to talk ye out of it."

Kerdik postured, miffed. "The Compass and the ability to hear unknown languages were both adequate blessings."

"Tha's not the one I'm talking about, and ye know it. The third blessing. I warned ye it would go south."

My breathing hitched, confused at the turn in the conversation. I had two birth blessings. No one ever mentioned a third. I tried to grab onto Link, and hoped the material I was fisting belonged to him. I was in two different places at once, and the sensation was completely disorienting.

Brìghde chuckled and tsked Kerdik. "It was a foolish blessing tha would only sink the poor babe. 'Tha she would only be as beautiful as she was kind' is a terrible weight to put on a person. Either she'd be a shrewd and capable ruler and dreadful to look upon, or she'd be gorgeous, and would get pushed over at the slightest opposition. Ye cursed her Kerdik. Ye cursed her, and then had the nerve to call it a blessing." Brìghde let out a loud laugh. "And then ye go falling in love with her? Let me guess, she's as kind as they come, and she'll sink Avalon when push comes to shove."

I could feel Kerdik's anger rising up. "For living as long as you have, you know nothing about the Fae you rule over. Kindness isn't a weakness. My Rose is not weak. She's survived much cruelty, and still manages to be gracious. She rules with her father, using her kindness as an asset – something you will never understand. Avalon is thriving under her rule, and though she is kind, she's withstood a civil war already, and came out standing tall – beautiful as ever."

"Oh, I understand a great many things, dear Kerdik. So you found a woman you can't tear your eyes from. How lovely. And how stupidly brazen to come lord it in front of my face. I don't need to pretend tha I won't hurt her, like I did with Tara. Consider yourself put out of your misery. She'll be dead by morning. Don't say I never did anything for ye," she simpered with a snotty smile.

Kerdik held his ground. "You couldn't if you tried. She has my blood in her. I gave her a transfusion, so you cannot kill her now. I'm not sure anything can."

I gasped in time with Brìghde, afraid and confused. Too many thoughts raced through my brain, setting my mind whirling with wonder and worry. *When Kerdik roused me from the peluda attack, did I somehow become immortal?*

Brìghde blew out a loud raspberry. "You're too selfish to do tha. There's no way you'd give a mere lass a portion of yourself. Only I've ever done tha before, and it weakened me for days. Ye wouldn't weaken yourself for another. I know the pride in ye runs deep. Ye wouldn't humble your-self for anybody."

Kerdik's voice came out glum. "She already owns my heart. What do I care if she has a bit of my blood as well?"

Brìghde shook her head, vacillating between furious and amused. "Ye really have fallen in love. For some, it takes a lifetime for tha to happen. For ye? It took several, and it seems it's still all for naught. Poor, frustrated Kerdik."

Kerdik didn't appreciate being talked down to. "The Avalon Rose can't be killed by you. She can only die of natural causes, not from an attack by an immortal, or any Fae other than the Daughters of Avalon. Oh, but I know your tricks of mental torture. If you go after her or her family in any way, I'll destroy your land. I can access Faîte's lost magic whenever I please, and won't hesitate to unleash all the darkness I locked away if you come near her. I came here because I knew you'd find out one way or another, and you'd go after Rosie. I'm telling you today that if one hair on her head is ruffled, or anyone near her, I'll take Éireland's lost magic, and set it loose on your people." He chuckled, and the sound was a brand of psychotic that made my spine shiver. "Oh, the hazards of having a heart that bleeds for your people. You should take a page from my book, and let them burn each other just to have done with it all."

Brìghde froze. "You're bluffing. Ye wouldn't risk any of the darkness bleeding into Avalon. No matter what ye say, ye don't want your land tarnished. It's not love tha drives ye, it's pride. Ye take pride when Avalon flourishes. Ye wouldn't devastate your own land just to destroy mine."

"That you still underestimate me just goes to show that you never knew the man you let into your bed."

Her lips pursed, but she seemed to swallow any tart reply that might spew out, and stuck to the greater issue. "We need the higher magic to stay gone. There's too much darkness there. Do ye want Vampires and Werewolves prowling about? Do ye think the Fae can handle flight and invisibility again? It would be nonstop chaos."

"Indeed. Which is why it would be foolish of you to go after my Rosie, unleashing Darkness, Violence and Evil just to spite me."

Brìghde deflated. "Cailleach has said for a long time tha the higher magic leaving the land was the best thing the three of us ever did."

"Indeed. The old hag is wise, I'll give her that. Rosie has too much magic protecting her. It's set to attack if any immortal tries to kill her – loaded like a spring to cut the hands off any little Éirish rats that try to gnaw at her. I hope you appreciate the courtesy I'm giving you by issuing this warning." Then his green hand reached out and grabbed Brìghde, crashing her to his chest. "I should be able to touch her how I please, when she finally outgrows the mortal she has affections for now. Undo my curse, Brìghde. Let me be with Rosie without fear of turning her into a monster."

Brìghde seemed to lose her resolve, panicking at the

new information that made her lose her upper hand. "I can't! Cailleach did the spell," she admitted, ashamed that her sister had done her homework for her. "I don't know how it works, much less how to undo it. It was Cailleach who cursed ye."

Kerdik released Brìghde with a huff of disgust. "Your hag will never give me what I need. Get her to undo it!"

"No! If anything, I'm saving tha poor lass from your affections." With the tears of a jilted woman dotting her face, she cried out, "You're toxic, Kerdik! You'll destroy her, with or without my curse. So much the better if she comes undone at your hands. It'd be just like ye to obliterate the thing ye love. Everything ye touch withers."

Brìghde's face disappeared when a hard slap across my cheek brought me back to my bedroom. Link alternated between slapping me and shaking my shoulders, a look of terror plain on his face. When my eyes focused on him, he exhaled loudly. "What was tha? Where did ye go? How do ye know about Brìghde?"

It took a few tries, but eventually I was able to push myself up to sitting. My chest heaved as I tried to put the world I was living currently in its proper order. I was in Lane's palace with Link. To my left, Jean-Luc had come in however long ago, and was shouting with his mouth closed. His muted words rang like a bell in my ears. *"Princess! Did you see her? Where is she? Where is Brìghde?"*

I rubbed my temples and slumped against Link's unin-jured shoulder, since it was closest. He rubbed my back in movements too jerky and rapid to be comforting. "Was all that real? Where's Kerdik right now?"

My father's voice was deep with worry, and came toward me from the doorway, which was to my back. "I sent him away, so you could have some space. He was going to try and lure the Sluagh away, and then take some time away from Province 9. Are you hurt?"

I shook my head, confused as to which rabbit hole I'd fallen down this time. "I was Kerdik. I mean, I was saying his words and seeing through his eyes. He's meeting with some Brìghde woman. She's... She's not too happy to see him."

My dad swore, which I'd never heard him do before. "I should've suspected he was more serious about you than he let on. Rosie, you're not to be alone with Kerdik ever again. I mean it. You have no idea what could happen to you."

"I know, I know. Brìghde and Cailleach cursed him, so that when he has sex, it turns the woman into a dragon. He told me already." I winced at the gasps that sounded from Link and Jean-Luc. "Maybe that was supposed to be private information. Sorry, guys. Keep that to yourselves. I'm a little turned around right now." I leaned more securely into Link's beefy shoulder, grateful he'd loaned me his unmarred one, so I could bury my face there until I felt a little steadier. "You don't have to worry about that, Dad. I'm with Bastien, and Kerdik knows that."

"You overestimate Kerdik's patience. And now he's

trying to undo his curse? He's doing it for you! Don't you see that?"

"Don't yell at me!" I countered. "Did anyone here just have a psychic conversation with two deities? No? Only me? That's what I thought. Give a girl a minute to catch up. Where I'm from? That's not normal, and I'm trying not to freak out here."

Link pressed his wide palm to my spine, which finally calmed me enough to pull in a deep breath. "Easy, lass. One step at a time. Where were they?"

"Where's Bastien?" I countered, wishing any of my true touchstones were here. Bastien had started to become someone I trusted, and Lane and Judah had earned that rite long ago. "Anyone get word on them? Have they found Lane and everyone yet?"

"Not yet, but tha's not unusual. They're probably getting to the castle now. The westward trip isn't too harrowing."

My gut screamed at me. "Westward? Did you say they headed west?"

"Aye. Your mammy's castle is west."

I stiffened and scrambled to my feet. "But they're not west. Lane's dead east. I mean, I can feel her." I patted my gut twice to indicate that my Compass was very much on the ball.

Urien's hand on my elbow led me to my bed so I could sit down, in case I got a case of the Kerdiks again. "I don't understand. Morgan's note said she was holding them in her dungeon, and to bring you and the ring for an exchange. Morgan's castle is west from here."

Dread painted my features, and regret hit me for the millionth time that I could not read a simple note. "I didn't check my gut. I didn't even think to ask my Compass where Lane was, and measure it against what the letter said. I should've been on top of this," I said with a cringe that affected my whole body. "Lane's not there. She's east. I'd bet her life on it." I hated the next words that tumbled out of my mouth, but someone had to say it. "The guys are headed for a trap."

9

A PRESIDENTIAL SENDOFF

"Tell me again how you talked me into this," Urien grumbled. His head only came up to my knee, now that I was mounted on a tall, brown horse.

"We don't have a military force set up yet, and I'm the only one who can figure out how to find Lane. You've got no choice, Dad." I added the paternal moniker to soften him, which it did.

The hard edge in his eyes gentled, and he gazed up at me with a fierce protectiveness. It was how I'd always wished my father would look on me. "Stay with Link," he warned us both.

"Aye, your majesty." We were both sucking up. Link didn't have to use the formal title, since he was Untouchable. He chose to add in the extra respect so my dad wouldn't freak out so much. "I've got both eyes on her. Nowhere safer than with an Untouchable."

"Yes, I keep telling myself that. It feels wrong not sending you out with more than these few men. Twelve of you? That's hardly enough to stand against Morgan."

"It's all we've got," I ruled. "Any more, and we won't be able to travel as quickly, or be as stealthy as we need."

"And I don't like you traveling without a ladies' maid. It's not proper."

I shrugged. "Link is my ladies' maid. He's super way awesome at braiding hair."

Link jerked his thumb to his chest. "Super way awesome, sire."

Urien cast Link a skeptical squint, and motioned for the eleven men to clear out so he could speak to me privately. "You've got your canteen?"

I smirked at his cuteness. "You sound like Lane whenever she sent me off for summer camp. I've got my canteen, Daddy." He could see it plain as day, hanging off my saddle.

"And you've got enough food in your pack?"

"Enough for the journey there and back, plus extra for everyone we bring home."

"Yes, this is your home. I'm your home, so make sure you return to me in one piece." Dad's eyes blazed into mine, and for the first time, I realized we didn't have the same eye color anymore. One of my irises was pink now. At least the other one matched. I don't know why it bummed me out that I looked slightly less his; I guess I was hoping that everything about us would always match.

"I'll come home to you, Dad. I'll be back before you know it. I've got an idea that might help the people have better access to fresh water, which would mean they'd fight over the wells less often. And make sure you have someone you trust checking in the new immigrants who wander to our borders. Make sure our guys aren't collecting tariffs. The newcomers have been through enough. They should feel welcome here, not like all they are is a dollar sign to us." The four of us had agreed on once a year tariffs, but we'd caught one of the men at the gates, who was supposed to be welcoming people and taking a census, collecting entry fees and pocketing them. Not cool to be a d-bag in Avalon. Dad had him hanged, which was his right, though I'd put up a fuss about it when it all went down. "Might want to post a sign or something."

"Consider it done."

"Oh, and if Gustav says he needs money to buy flour for the free bread he's supposed to be providing for anyone in need, give him flour, not money."

"As you wish. That was good advice, dear."

"I have my moments. And the women who've been snubbed by the province for being left by their men? I gave the list of their names to Aimee. While I'm gone, and she's got some free time, could you send her out with some macarons or something from the kitchen to take to them? There's thirty-seven women who've been shunned. By the time I get back, I'd love to see that number ratcheted down to zero."

"I adore you and your heart. I'll send Aimee out first thing."

We were still getting to know each other, so I was never sure if I was supposed to hug him, kiss his cheek, or high-five him. As I was on the horse, I settled for reaching out my hand, my heart swelling as he clasped my palm between his two beefy ones. My hand felt small in his, which for some reason put my worries at ease. If Superman was bigger than the things that clawed at me, then maybe we had a chance. "Could you tell Pascal that I..." I swallowed hard. I'd gone with my father to deliver the terrible news, along with Montel's body. Pascal's lined face had contorted into sheer horror and devastation that his only boy was no more. I went along so Pascal could have the chance to curse me to my face – Montel had died guarding me, after all. But Pascal shocked me to my core by thanking me for killing the Sluagh, so his son's spirit could be released to rest in the afterlife.

I didn't understand how someone could have the presence of mind to be gracious in that scenario, but I learned a lot in that short exchange. Pascal knew who he was, and not even his entire world being ripped from him could change that. Though truly, I think I would've preferred he yelled at me. Then his voice could replace the shouting I was doing at myself.

"Now, when you find Lane and the others, make sure you stay back. Let Link go in and get them," Urien instructed.

I nodded, though we both knew I was incapable of falling back when I should be charging forward. "Tell me it gets better," I begged quietly.

My horse and my dad replied in unison, "It gets far better." Urien kissed my knuckles, his trimmed mustache and short beard scraping sweetness over my skin. "One day, I'll show you Avalon as you've never known."

"I love you, Dad."

"Don't say it like that," he pleaded, his eyes closed. "Don't say it like you're not coming back to me."

He was afraid, which struck me in waves of preciousness and terror. If my dad was afraid, then did we stand a chance? What state would we find Lane and them in when we got there? "Okay," I nodded, humoring him. "See you in a few days. When I get back, we're totally playing baseball together. You'll love it." I lowered my voice and cleared my throat, glancing around to make sure no one could eavesdrop. "Dad, did you know about my third birth blessing?"

His mouth drew in a tight line. "I did not. No one did. Kerdik must've done that in secret. Though, it's no wonder you've become the most beautiful woman in the land. Your kindness is legendary." His eyes sparkled with unshed tears, and I knew if I didn't get out of there, I'd have blood streaking down my cheeks, which wasn't something I wanted the guys I was traveling with to learn about me. I patted my horse's mane and spoke with authority to iron out the quaver I knew would come if I didn't buck up. "Come on, Daisy," I said to my horse. Her name was actually Coureur Par La Mer Qui Est Rapide, plus about three more syllables I couldn't remember. She hated her name, so we decided on Daisy. It felt like Bastien was riding with me, which gave me a little more confidence.

Daisy cantered out to where the twelve men were waiting with their chins high and eyes on my dad, who exited the barn behind me. His voice raised to the team, whose chests all broadened at being addressed by their king. "If all else fails, return the Avalon Rose to me unbroken." He waved his hand, sending us off in presidential style. I felt like Eowyn on her steed in *Lord of the Rings*, running headfirst into danger without a blink.

10

GIRL TALK WITH LINK

The excitement of the chase didn't die down until the men realized that me sleeping was nonnegotiable. I rode for as long as I could through the province and out into no man's land, but Daisy was a chatterbox. She'd lived an exciting life thus far, and wanted to impart every piece of wisdom onto me, including where I should sleep, and the softest spots I should lay. I knew she was steadily running down my internal battery, but after being cooped up with Walter for so long, Daisy was a breath of fresh air I couldn't pass up.

Three of the men went out to hunt up some dinner, while I tried to make myself a little nest to sleep the night away. I was grateful that some of the animals in Avalon also required rest, otherwise I would've pushed myself to stay awake until I fell clean off my horse.

"Here, Rosie. Have some dinner before ye lie down."

I leaned against Daisy's back, smiling when the twelve other horses sat in a ring around me to keep the men out. "It's alright, guys. Link's cool. You can let him in."

Link bristled as he strode into the fold. "Tha's right. Fickle horse," he chided his own steed, who snorted at him in response for being too heavy. Link sat down in the dirt beside me, handing me a chunk of hard cheese, a dinner roll, and a cluster of grapes. "Want me to wake ye when they come back with the kill?"

"No, thanks. This is more than enough food for me." I looked up at the sky and marveled at the expanse of stars that seemed almost like a disco ball, all spread out up there. Each point of light seemed peaceful up there, looking down on our chaos with bemused complacency. I drew a small amount of solace from their tranquility so high above us. If our world couldn't be a safe place, at least there was hope for the celestial orbs in the heavens to get along. I pointed to a particularly gorgeous twinkle above us that seemed to wink at me, as if we were sharing some inside joke. "That's the one thing Avalon's got on Common. We have a ton of light pollution, so we don't get a good view of the sky. I can't believe how many stars you've got here. Plus that blue moon? Ours is white. Yours is way cool."

"The *one* thing Avalon's got on Common? Avalon's got me, for now at least. Tha's something Common's lacking."

"Plus that, of course. All the ladies in Common are no

doubt crying themselves to sleep every night, because they don't get to see your magnificent smile."

Link flashed me his playboy grin. "Wouldn't hurt ye to say it once in a while."

"You're the king of every girl's dreams," I offered, tapping the outside of my boot to his.

"Yours too?"

"Oh, of course. I'm all like, 'who cares about Bastien?' All the ladies love Link."

He sniggered. "Cheers, Rosie."

"Who was the best kiss of your life?" I asked as we munched together.

Link grinned and laid back on Daisy, who grudgingly accommodated his weight after I vouched for him. "Ah, tha's not easy, now. I never put much stock in kissing. Best lay of my life? Tha's a better question."

"Hit me with it. Who'd you lose your Cocoa Puffs for?"

"Mae," he cooed wistfully. "Now she was a beaut. Big cherry lips. Legs for days. Woman from head to toe. She had melons bigger than yours, even."

I scoffed, crossing an arm over my chest. "You're not allowed to think about my melons, for the record."

"Can't ignore prizes tha big," he teased. "I'm only kidding. But Mae was incredible. Bossed me around in the bedroom. I didn't think I would like tha, but boy, did I. Most lasses get so overwhelmed when we tumble in the hay, tha I do most of the work. I'm not complaining, but

Mae knew what she wanted, and made me beg for what I needed."

"She sounds fun."

"Aye, she was. Haven't thought about her in ages." He wrapped his arm around my shoulders when I yawned. "How about ye? Is Bastien the prettiest lad you've ever laid eyes on?" Link batted his lashes at me, trying his hand at girl talk.

"He's a keeper, that's for sure. He's more of an explosion. When we kiss, I don't know which way's up. I've only kissed two other guys in my life, so I don't have much to compare it to. Still, he bowled me over from the very first kiss, and probably long before that."

"Tha's good to hear. He's not really the explosion type of lad. To watch him get swept away by ye? Tha was a sight to see."

I yawned again, and sat up to stretch as I swallowed the last of my dinner. "I think I'm gonna turn in, so, you know, scram."

"Sleep away, but ye don't leave my side. The lads can watch the perimeter well enough while I guard ye."

"Link, you don't have to do that. I've worked on the wall with everyone here. They're all cool."

"It's sweet tha ye think ye have a choice in the matter. If I ever lost my mind and settled down, I'd expect Bastien to do the same for my lady. Shut your eyes, wee Rose. I'll watch out for ye." Link snuggled me closer to him, so my head rested on his shoulder. He was leaning back on Daisy, providing me with a comfortable place to rest.

Some days, that's the very definition of a great friend.

My arm wrapped around his middle, giving him a light squeeze of gratitude. "Goodnight, Link."

He kissed my forehead, making me feel treasured and safe. We'd left the comfort of our province long ago, and had been riding through land that belonged to no one now, the scenery getting less green the further we went. I was acutely aware of how exposed we were without the cover of enough trees to keep us hidden from the shadows. Though I wanted to assure him and myself that I didn't need to be guarded while I slept, a knot in my chest loosened when Link held me tighter in the quiet of the evening. "Goodnight, wee Rose."

My eyes drifted shut while the men kindled a fire a stone's throw away. Daisy and the other horses had worn me out in a way I hadn't been exhausted in a while. Walter hadn't liked to talk to me, so I'd only been able to take short naps when I was locked in the saferoom with him. It wasn't long before the crackle of the fire and the dull murmurs from the guys lulled me to sleep.

11

THE REMNANTS OF A PROVINCE LONG GONE

It wasn't unheard of in Avalon for whole sections of the land to remain untouched after the famine swept through when a Jewel of Good Fortune deserted a province. Still, traveling through the empty Province 4 was a sadness that couldn't be capped. A holy hush fell over us, and even the horses understood that the bramble and dried-out bushes we passed were not to be disturbed.

Province 4 had belonged to my late cousin Roland, who died because he attacked me. Not enough of his people were willing to leave the comfort of Province 1 to make his land strong enough to stand on its own. After his death, they didn't have a leader anymore. It was a prudent move to join forces with Lane, merging the provinces so we could stand more boldly in front of Morgan. Now they had a duchess to fight for them, which they were all grateful for. Still, to lose a whole state's-worth of land like this was a hit none of us took lightly.

One of the soldiers, Marcus, stopped his horse and dismounted. We all followed suit, watching as he scooped up a fistful of hard dirt and sprinkled it in his pack. There was a hard look in his eyes as he surveyed the area. I didn't need to ask him which province he'd come from; it was clearly Province 4 his heart still belonged to.

The man next to him placed his hand on Marcus' shoulder, and something about the reminder of support set his tongue loose. "This land could've been thriving and bursting with life. Duke Roland got the Jewel of Good Fortune back. I saw this place not more than a handful of memories ago. It was a home we took pride in, and it welcomed us with open arms when we dragged our families here, tired of Morgan's abuse. I wish more of us had believed in him. I wish more of us had stood up against Morgan le Fae when Duke Roland came back to claim us. But now..." His gaze took in the same desolation we did. There were rotting trees, no wildlife, and a dried pit where I'm guessing a river had once been off in the distance. Even the mountains we were riding near seemed to have a "get out now" kind of M.O. to them.

The soldier who still had his hand on Marcus' shoulder tried to speak peace into the inner tumult. "This land will be ours once again. The Avalon Rose will defeat Morgan le Fae. We have King Urien now. Have faith, friend. Avalon will unite before the end."

"Before whose end?" Marcus asked without blinking, searching out solace in the bramble. "So much of me feels gone with my homeland."

Marcus was drawn into a hug by his friend, and we all bowed our heads, observing the sadness with a respectful silence for the wars that had taken too much from us all.

I swallowed hard, unsure how I felt about the grand hope being that I would end my own mother. I mean, of course we couldn't let her keep going on unchecked, but what power did I really have? I could affect policies, sure, and I did my best to raise Province 9 up on steady ground that would hold true for all of us. Aside from that, though, I didn't have many other plans. I didn't know how to over-throw Morgan. Is that what they were all expecting me to do? Was I supposed to be coming up with some sort of plan? We were just trying to get our region functional for now. My fingers twisted in the hem of my shirt, and I wondered just what kind of insanity might have to possess me to storm her castle, or whatever the expectation was. I'd barely made it out alive the first time, and didn't relish the notion of going back.

Link reached over and held onto my hand to stop my fingers from twisting in the fabric of the hem of my tank top. "Best not worry about it all right now," Link promised in a whisper. "No matter what the people say, it won't come down to you having to murder your mammy."

I gulped up at him, worried that it very well might. I didn't know how to ask for what I needed, and wasn't sure he could give it to me anyway. I wanted the Untouchables to stay with me, to make sure the nation we were precariously reassembling would hold under Morgan's wrath. I wasn't sure *I* could stand strong under her special brand of cruelty.

People often write off the court jester, but I'd always known Link was wiser than penis jokes and goofball antics. He squeezed my hand, and as if he could read my mind, he pulled me closer and spoke low in my ear. "We'll stay with ye until ye send us away. T'won't do for ye to get a crown, and then have it so quickly snatched away."

I didn't have the words, so I snuggled into Link's side to show him my gratitude.

Link kissed the top of my head with affection he didn't bother to conceal from the men. "The Brotherhood won't abandon our sister to ruin. I'll stay with ye while ye figure this whole mess out."

"I love you, Link," I finally worked out. "Thank you."

I could hear the smile in his voice. "Right ye are to love me. I'm adorable."

A few hours into our trek through Province 4, Marcus had pepped up a bit and volunteered to be our tour guide. "Over here is where the dance hall used to be. Every Saturday night when I was a boy, there was music to fill the whole square. They would start playing, and by the end of the first song there would be wall-to-wall people, crammed in to get a little lightness through the night."

"What kind of songs did they play?" I asked as I cantered beside him.

I expected him to answer with folk music, or if I was lucky, gangster rap. I startled when Marcus belted out a loud, operatic tune that was just lively enough to dance to. "'Never, not ever have I seen a land as ripe and as lovely as four. Nothing, no nothing could tell those sweet mountains to bow to neighboring shores.'" Then he went in for the chorus, not holding back for the groans of the horses, who didn't have the same taste in music as Marcus. "'The light in the sun is a lantern to some when compared with Province 4!'"

The men clapped politely, but Marcus had been so passionate in his opera that I hooted and cheered as if I was at a Lost and Forgotten concert (which, incidentally, I had gone to with Judah once, and we screamed ourselves hoarse).

Marcus tipped his head to us, his cheeks pinking when he bowed his chin at me. "Thank you, Princess."

"When we get back, remind me to ask around to see if there are any musicians. I think that's a great idea, having a music night for people to flock to. Once a week, dance your brains out and get crazy. I like that. Good idea, Marcus."

Marcus spluttered as his chest puffed with pride. "Your majesty, I didn't mean to suggest anything should change about your kingdom. Everyone is just happy to be free. Your lovely face is all the music they need."

I balked at him, and let out a nervous laugh. "Okay,

sweet as that is, it's a bunch of baloney. Music night. First thing when we get back. Where do you think? Is there a building big enough, or should we just have it in Town Square?"

"Town Square," one of the other men ruled.

One of the others countered the idea. "But what if the weather's foul?"

I grinned back at them with hope that optimism and play hadn't been beaten out of them over the years. "Then we'll be the province that dances in the rain. In fact, I think that's exactly who we should be."

The men cheered, and something about the wildness of it all drove the horses a little faster, bringing smiles to each of our faces.

It wasn't until after a few minutes of the breeze whipping through our hair that the smiles broke. The sound of one of the men and his horse cried out, making us all turn to investigate the problem. Daisy and I slowed with the others, turning to find one of the horses crying out on ground, writhing in frustration. *"It's the Caisse D'épines! Run!"* she whinnied.

"What's the Caisse D'épines?"

The men cried out in alarm at my words, jerking their horses to move further away from the injured one. Link was the only one who seemed to understand the situation, and was able to stay on top of it. "Soldier, hop on with one of us. Everyone else, ride ahead as fast as ye can! Go!"

I didn't have it in me to ride away and leave this dude. I

trotted Daisy over to him, wondering what the crap Caisse D'épines actually was, but knowing this wasn't the time to ask. I gasped when I saw vines camouflaged in with the dirt, wrapped around the felled horse's ankles. She cried for me to help her, so I hopped off of Daisy and drew my knife to cut her free.

Link jerked me away from the brown, ropey plants that tightened painfully around the horse's ankles. "No! Rosie, get back on your horse! If the vines get ye, there'll be no getting back up!"

"But she's stuck!" I balked, confused as to how Link could just leave the horse like this. "If we don't help her, she'll die out here!"

Link's voice held the edge of a command to it. I realized that on this trip, he was the captain, and I was being insubordinate. "On your horse, Rosie!" he ordered with trepidation plain on his face.

The abandoned horse whinnied in agony as I turned my back on her, and my morals. The long sound of defeat and woe shook my bones as she called out into the fading daylight, telling the barren land about the plight that had befallen her as her ankles were crushed.

12

CAISSE D'ÉPINES

The soldier who'd lost his horse to the Caisse D'épines was named Wyatt. He wasted no time hoisting me back on my horse. Then he climbed on behind me with a fearful expression on his face. "Hurry, Princess!" He took the reins and snapped them, jerking us forward, with Link at our side.

"What the crap is going on?" I winced at the sound of the fallen horse's desperation. We were leaving the injured mare to ruin, and all Daisy could think of was that she was grateful it hadn't been her.

"Faster!" Link ordered, and I knew he was keeping our pace so as not to leave us behind. Daisy chugged as fast as she could, but a quick getaway was just plain harder with two people on your back than only one.

"Link, we can't leave her like that! She'll die!"

Link didn't answer me, but spoke to Wyatt. "Don't stop

until the sun sets. I mean it. Don't slow for nothing. If we saw one Caisse D'épines, there are others hiding out there."

"Yes, Captain. Quick feet are our only hope."

I wanted to demand answers, but all of a sudden, something burst out from the ground ahead of us, shooting up into the air at least three stories high. It was a branchless, brown tree trunk with dozens of spindly vines that hooked out like tentacles, snatching at the air, as if in search of a tasty treat. Daisy shrieked in time with me, but didn't rear up, thank goodness. She obeyed Wyatt, who recovered quickly and veered right. Link darted left after his horse spooked.

I screamed when another tree trunk burst through the dirt in our path, driving us further to the right. I didn't understand what these things were, and knew this wasn't the time to ask questions.

"Take the reins, your grace!" Wyatt said, pulling his sword from its sheath. "Steer us toward the others, if you can. I'll defend us if one of the vines should strike."

"On it!" I cried, grateful I could be useful through the foreign situation. I took the reins in my trembling hands and tried to steer Daisy with a calm that might make her trust me. I wanted to communicate that this would all be okay. It was a good lie, and she pretended she bought it.

The vines went berserk from the tops of the mammoth trunks, moving like agile and ambitious octopus tentacles – alien and unpredictable in their paths.

I tried to keep my focus, zeroing in on the others, who weren't all that far off. They were riding towards a gap in the mountains, and I wondered if the plan was to flit through and hide on the other side. I tried to think of it all as a video game, with stakes no higher than Judah doing his obnoxious victor's dance if I lost. I tried not to gulp at my impending death, or that of the man whose life I was now responsible for. We dodged too many narrow misses, but Daisy obeyed, not losing her focus as we closed in on our goal.

I nearly cried when Daisy flitted through the gap between the two mountains. The others were catching their breath, grateful to see us returned to them.

Except we weren't all here. "Where's Link?"

"He's still coming, your grace," Marcus answered gravely.

"Hop on off, Wyatt. You alright?"

Wyatt obeyed, sheathing his sword before dismounting. "I'm well. Thank you for the rescue."

I nodded, but barely heard anything else. I turned Daisy around and went back to the entrance. The men were walled in by two gray masses of rock that assured me the guys would be safe until the vine monsters chilled out. My eyes scanned the landscape for signs of Link, who should've been right behind us.

When movement caught my eye, it wasn't Link on his horse, but simply my Untouchable, running for all he was worth from too far away. I swore, not thinking it all the way through as I called over my shoulder for the others to stay where they were. They cried out in earnest for me to stay with them. A few trotted over to me, and I knew if I didn't go now, they'd block my path. "We've got to get Link," I told Daisy, warning her before I snapped the reins.

13

NOTHING YOU COULD SAY COULD TEAR ME AWAY FROM MY GUY

My horse didn't want to go back for Link, but she didn't dare disobey. I didn't know a whole ton about the land, but I knew that Link didn't stand a chance, running instead of riding. A warrior to his core, Link ran with an expressionless determination to get to safety, no matter what monster chased him down. He was still a football field away, and there was a vine monster in his path, but that didn't stop him. That seemed to be the way with the Untouchables.

Daisy was warning me to turn us back, but I couldn't leave Link to fend for himself. Bastien had gone to rescue my Lane. I couldn't let him come home to a dead Link. That thought sent a chill up my spine. What kind of a world would this be without Link to make us laugh? What would be the point of rebuilding if such a goofy soul was destroyed out here, in the middle of nowhere? I kept Bastien tight in my heart, vowing to myself that he wouldn't lose another friend. Roland had been enough of a blow, but I knew he wouldn't get back up if Link was taken from him. I couldn't begin to imagine how Madigan would function without Link. People underestimate the value of play. They'll fight for rights and freedom easily enough, but fighting for the ability to play is just as important. If I let Daisy talk me out of this, or if I'd listened to the soldiers' cries for me to stay back with them, the best smile in all of Éireland might cease to exist.

I couldn't imagine a more tragic loss.

Link shouted at me to turn around, but I didn't obey. I didn't slow until he was close enough to get on the horse behind me. He hopped on, his hands trembling as his arms wound around my waist. "You're mad! Tha's foolish, Rosie! Ye don't come back out when there's a Caisse D'épines on the loose!"

"I love you!" I replied simply as I dug my heels into Daisy's sides. She didn't need the prodding, though. She took off back toward the others with lightning speed (or, you know, a horse's speed). Her voice was a steady stream of worries that we wouldn't make it back to our hidey hole between the mountains. When another mammoth trunk split the ground not ten feet from where we were, I was starting to wonder if she might be right.

I held on tight, Link's arms caging me in as he gripped my hands that held the reins. We rode hard and fast around the trunks that were thicker than the length of

Daisy's body. The vines spun every which way as they swung down toward us, swooping in our path and grabbing at us with a ferocity that pushed a scream out of my mouth. I could no longer convince myself that I was in a video game.

Link bent his upper half over mine, smooshing my chest to Daisy so we were more aerodynamic. It wasn't until he cried out with an agonized "Ah!" that I realized he was shielding me with his body, taking the beating so I didn't have to.

Link held on tighter now, and I could tell he was in pain. He was breathing through gritted teeth, and letting out low growls and grunts with every turn we made to dodge the vine beasts.

I don't think anyone would've judged me if I burst into tears when we finally crossed through the gap into safety, but I couldn't break down until I saw the scope of the damage that had been inflicted on my friend. He dismounted with a noise of distress, and fell to his knees, leaning over on all fours like a dog as he panted through the pain.

My legs were rubbery, and I tripped after I got my leg out of the stirrup. Wyatt steadied me and offered me a drink from his canteen. "Easy, easy. I can't believe you did that."

Marcus was white with fear. "Your majesty, if you die, the kingdom perishes! You can't go throwing yourself into..." He caught himself mid-lecture, realizing that scolding me wasn't his place.

I indulged in a few swallows, but pushed the canteen away so I could get to Link. "He's hurt!" I said in a wobbly voice. I needed Link not to ever get a papercut. I needed the Untouchables to have a life of fluffy pillows and candies at every turn. I needed them to never have a bad day, a stubbed toe, or you know, a wallop across the back from a tree monster.

I dropped down next to him and started to peel off his shirt. My fingers trembled as they skated over his skin, taking in the foot-wide mark that stretched across his entire massive back. The others gasped at his scars, most of which had been tattooed over. The zipper designs went every which way on his body, making him look like he was constantly being unzipped, and his innards might spill out.

"What can I do?" I asked him quietly, worried that we hadn't thought to travel with a healer.

"Get the lads away," he whispered, his words coming out through gritted teeth.

I raised my shaking voice just a little to be heard. "Is everyone here? We all made it?"

Marcus answered for the group. "Yes, your majesty. We lost two horses, but other than that, we're okay."

"Good. Awesome job, guys. Marcus, can the tree monsters get at us if we stay behind these mountains?"

"No, your majesty. They can't cross pure rock of this size."

"If we're safe here, then let's break for the night. The horses need to rest, and we wouldn't get much farther now anyways, since it'll be dark soon. Go on over there, so I can talk with Link, alright?" I was usually more diplomatic, but the narrow escape had made me slightly more direct.

"Yes, your majesty. Only make sure you don't linger near the gap. It's possible for one of the vines to snake through."

"Thanks, man." When the others left for an area a safe distance from us with the horses, I positioned my body between Link's and the gap, knowing he wasn't ready to move just yet.

"Go on," Link said, his eyes on the rocky dirt as he remained on all fours. "I'll catch up."

"Okay," I replied, with no intention of obeying. I remained by his side, silent through the echoes of his pain.

His panting grew more uneven, and I wondered if he might faint. His skin was covered in a thin sheen of sweat, showing off the divots in his flesh from his many scars. Beneath the relief of our safety, a deep sadness washed over me, replacing a bit of my optimism that I needed to survive. I needed to be able to hold my head up and believe that everything would somehow be okay. Seeing deep abuse like Link's? It took away a little of that belief in the goodness that kept me from hardening over. Link was my sweetie pie, and yet, he'd been worked over and sliced open too many times to count.

"Go on," Link repeated, still gripping the ground through waves of pain.

"I did. I'm over there with the guys right now," I lied lamely.

"They can't see me like this. We're unstoppable. They need to believe tha. They need to see us as something tha keeps them safe, otherwise they have nothing. Don't let them see me, Rosie."

It was the same logic that made me stay inside until the beak-marks had mostly faded on my body. If the people saw me injured, they knew whatever bested me would aim at them next.

I glanced around and spotted a little divot in the mountain just a few yards away. "Can you move? There's a spot over there where you can take a breather."

"Aye." It took a few tries, but finally Link stood, grimacing with every step as I led him toward the private mini cove. It was just big enough for the two of us. I was careful with his body as I slowly lowered him to the ground. His muffled "oof!" didn't inspire much confidence in a speedy recovery, but he was able to move around, which was something. I quickly retracted my hands from his once he was in place, wary of the bite that always came when Bastien was wounded. If Link was anything like Bastien, the anger was still coming. Link looked up at me with a hard expression, so I braced myself. "Ye shouldn't have come back out."

"Okay." I replied simply, unwilling to fight about it.

"Next time a possessed tree tries to take you out, I'll just let you die." I lowered myself next to him, but kept a foot of space between us, the shade falling over my knees. "Can I have your fancy knife when you croak?"

Link snorted. "Ye want my knife?"

"Well, I was going to ask for your collection of fancy dresses, but I've already got enough of those. Plus, what else would we bury you in? I was thinking you could wear something pink and lacy when we put you in the ground for being prideful, not accepting help when it comes riding in on a horse to save you."

Link laughed, and the sound surprised me. I turned toward him, my eyes wide that he was capable of joy, and that he wasn't snapping at me for being near him when he was vulnerable. "Now tha's a good reason for me to stay out of harm's way. Are ye alright?"

"Are you serious? How are you even thinking about me right now? What can I do for your back?"

He waved off my concern as if he'd merely fallen off his skateboard. "Nothing. Just going to bruise up nasty by morning, is all. I might be a little stiff, so if ye plan on seducing me tonight, ye might have to be on top."

"Fair enough."

Link extended his arm, motioning for me to come in for a snuggle. "Tha's better," he said when I cuddled into his side, my hand on his chest to soothe his jumping heart. "Ye should've stayed back, where it was safe with the others."

"Okay."

"It was dangerous, what ye did."

"Okay."

Link sighed, and tightened his arm around me. "Ye saved my life. No way was I going to make it. When my horse went down, I barely got on my feet before the Caisse D'épines came after me. Nasty bugger." He shook his head, as if confused. "Ye risked your life to save me. Why?"

I blinked up at him, as if the reason for that should be obvious. "Because I love you. I thought you knew that."

"Aye, but *I'm* supposed to save *ye*, not the other way around."

"Okay, well then next time, it's your turn to rescue me."

"Bastien would never be the same if he lost ye."

"Hello, the same thing could be said if he lost you." I pulled back and tapped my neck tattoo, reminding us both of my ink. "I'm in the Brotherhood. You're my people. I would never leave someone I loved to fend for themselves. You think this means that I'm under your protection? Fine. It also means that you're under my protection."

Link gaped at me, as if the concept was foreign to him. When he finally spoke, he pulled me closer, positioning his legs so I was sitting between them, curled up against his wide chest. "Katya is Nicholai's lady. She has a thing for expensive clothes, but doesn't like to pay for them. One of the rights of the Untouchable is tha we don't have to pay for anything ever again. Still, we don't like to be tyrants and go around robbing people. So we take what we need, and tha's all. Katya takes full advantage of the privileges of being married to Nicholai. One of the seamstresses got her measurements wrong, so Katya went to the shop in a rage, showing off her tattoo and demanding the woman's hands be cut off for making such a big mistake."

I shuddered. "You're joking."

"I wish. Of course, we did no such thing. When I told her no, she picked up a pot and tried to whack me over the head with it."

"She sounds swell."

"Yeah. Nicholai drinks a lot."

"I'll bet."

Link ran his palm up and down my back slowly, as if we'd chosen this spot to decompress just for fun, not because we'd been chased here by a monster. "She'd do crazy things like stir up fights in the village, then send us in there to defend her honor – as if she had any."

"Dude, that sucks."

Link's arms tightened around my form. "Tha ye rode out to save me? It's true honor ye have, Rosie, and I'll defend ye till the end. People assume we don't need anyone to fight for us, but we do."

I turned in his arms when I picked up on the forlorn note of insecurity in his voice. Sitting up on my knees, I tugged him forward, so he could rest his forehead on my shoulder. His arms banded around my hips as he gave himself permission to breathe. "I'll always fight for you, Link. You're safe now. I've got you."

He exhaled into my neck, as if my words were the sweetest lullaby he'd ever heard. My hand trailed over his back, my fingers careful with his enormous burgeoning bruise. His head remained on my shoulder as my hands found their way to his arms, massaging his biceps, and working my way up. I rubbed his meaty shoulders, wondering when the last time was that he'd taken ten minutes to be kind to his body. Link groaned into my neck, deflating as I worked my way over the unbruised parts of him, massaging and letting him know that he wasn't alone in this. He didn't always have to be the strong one. I would take care of my Untouchables when they needed me.

Link still bore peck marks all over his arms from the Sluagh's ravens. They were fading, but visible all the same. Mine, on the other hand, had healed completely. I couldn't understand the discrepancy, especially since I'd been sliced many more times by their beaks than he had.

We stayed just like that in our tender hold until the sun started to set, and my yawn gave me away. "I think it's time for me to turn in," I admitted. "Can you get up yet?"

"Aye. Tha…" He sighed into my neck, his body a loose noodle as my fingertips stroked the hair at the nape of his neck. "Thanks, honey. I think I needed tha." He kissed my tattoo, drawing out a blush to my cheeks. He shivered as the slight breeze kissed the tiny hairs on his shoulders.

"You're cold. Let's get your shirt back on, sweetie." I took my time working the material over his head and threading his arms through.

"No one's dressed me since I was a wee lad," Link remarked with a bashful smile. "The ladies are always trying to get my clothes off me, not put them on."

I unrolled the hem over his torso, covering up the evidence of all that life had inflicted upon him. When I stood, I stared down at my adorable friend, brushing a few hairs off his forehead. "You sure you're alright? No ribs are broken?"

"Not a one."

It took a few tries, but eventually I got him to stand. Link did his best to posture as we walked together back to the others, but I noticed the tightness in his walk.

They'd built a fire as the night chill started to set in. I chose a spot near the horses to lie down away from the others. Link offered me the shirt he'd worn yesterday to use as a pillow. He grimaced, but got down on his knees next to me when I laid down near Daisy. "What are you doing? You don't need to miss out on guy time for this. I'll be fine, Link. Go have fun."

Link laid on his back, grunting as he tried to find a comfortable spot on the hard, rocky ground. "Not out of my sight. I promised your Da I'd keep ye safe. Tuck on in here and get some sleep."

I situated myself next to Link, curling into his side, and practically purring at the warmth he radiated. "Goodnight, Link. I love you." The words slipped easily from my lips. Though I knew I'd said them to him before, tonight they held a note of permanence – as if we were married, and said our nightly pledges to each other before bed.

"I love ye, too."

"Wake me if you need me to beat up any bad guys."

Link sniggered. "Aye. Rest well, wee Rose."

14

PIG AND BUCKET

"*Stop it! Let me go!*"

The squeal of panic roused me with a jolt. I startled against Link, who was sharpening his blade on a nearby rock with his one free hand. His other arm remained securely fashioned around me, and rubbed up and down when I woke. "Is tha all ye needed to sleep? It's barely been an hour."

"What? No. Link, we have to help her!"

"Who?" The space between his eyebrows puckered.

"*I have a family! Please!*"

I shrieked and scrambled to my feet, pulling the dagger my dad had given me from its sheath, ready to fend off whatever foe was bearing down on us. When no one else was on high alert and a few heads craned curiously in my direction, I assessed the situation anew. The three who'd left to go hunt up some dinner had returned, bringing back a pig who was tied up, and still very much alive. My shoulders deflated and I sheathed my knife. It was only then that I realized Link was standing behind me with his sword drawn. "Never mind. It's the pig," I explained, trying to be cool about it.

Link's eyebrows furrowed until realization dawned on him. "Ah, ye can hear her. What's she saying?"

I clenched my fist, my teeth on edge. "You don't want to hear it. It would ruin your supper."

"Let me go! Let me go! Help!"

My stomach churned as the pig broke free of its bindings and ran around, trying to dodge the men without much success. I sat back down next to Daisy, who was sound asleep, and covered my ears. I could still hear the panic, the sheer terror that the pig squealed through the night.

"My babies! My babies! They have no one else! You don't understand! Let me go! Monsters! You're monsters!"

She pled with them, tugging at my heartstrings and jerking tears from me as I rocked on the grass, my hands over my ears. "I'll make it quick," Link promised, running to the men to lend his sword to the mix.

"You're a monster! You're a monster! You're..." With a final screech, the pig said no more.

I knew it was weird to rock myself and sob over a pig being made into ham and bacon. I wasn't a preachy vegetarian by nature. It was the fact that I could hear them, understand their feelings, and that they could understand mine. It made the whole circle of life thing excruciating for me. I kept my sobs quiet, hiccupping into my hand until my vision clouded over with red. Then I knew my own personal brand of terror. I was in unknown territory, and I couldn't see. I couldn't blink away the gooey red that coated my eyes and face, and now my hands. I tried to wipe the mess away, but my tears couldn't be reasoned with. "Link!" I wailed, ashamed that a little upset could turn south so fast. "Link, help!"

I felt around on the grass like a blind person, willing to crawl my way to him if I had to. Link's boots pounded the earth, cursing when I turned my face toward him. "The princess is alright, mates. Go back to the fire, and leave us be. Now! No one look at her!"

I didn't know what to do, so I curled myself into a ball and pressed my face to the earth, praying the grass would conceal my inhuman traits. Bloody tears would surely lend themselves to rumors and much speculation. "Link!" I whimpered, scared that I couldn't see a thing in the middle of a land I didn't know well enough to go through blind.

Link dropped to his knees and draped his heavy arm over my body, shielding me with his broad shoulders. "Shh. Make it stop, Rosie! I don't know how to calm ye down!"

I cried into my hands, catching more blood that dripped between my fingers and sprinkled onto the grass. "I can't make it stop! I'm a freak now!"

Link gripped my shoulders and shook me, as if that

was how to calm a crying woman. Something told me it was a good thing that he and Mae had shared a strictly bedroom relationship. "Make it be over! There, there? The pig's dead now, yeah?"

I cried harder, mourning the babies she'd had that would most likely die, now that their mother was gone. "I can't see!" I sobbed, clutching the grass on all fours, like an animal I prayed the world would have mercy upon.

When shaking me and yelling at me didn't make the tears go away, Link was at his wit's end. In a hurried and quiet voice, he started singing frantically to me, rushing through the lyrics. "'In the dark of night, my eyes can find ye. My eyes can find your heart wherever it roams. There's nothing in all of Faîte that could separate us. 'Cause wherever ye lay your head, I'll find my new home.'"

My tears stopped in time with my shock, as if turning off a faucet. "D-did you just make that up? That was beautiful." I scrubbed at the red goo that painted my face. Now that I wasn't adding more tears by the second, I was able to wipe away enough so that I could see Link through a crimson film.

Link shushed me, and then darted his chin over his shoulder. He looked worried he'd be caught being sweet, and then swiftly ostracized by the dudes. "Shut your gob about it. I didn't make it up. My mammy used to sing it to me every night while she tucked me in when I was a wee lad."

"That's such a sweet song. Thank you."

"Is tha shutting up about it?"

"You have a gorgeous voice."

"Rosie, I swear."

I swallowed thickly, trying to get my head on straight. "Do we have any water? I have to wash my face. I can barely see you."

"Aye. Hold on, ye blind, bloody beauty." He grabbed his canteen from the provisions and wetted his palm so he could scrub my face. I braced myself on all fours, and let the water drip down my nose and chin. I was afraid of the blood staining my clothes, making me look like I'd been stabbed so early on in our journey. Link wiped down my sopping face with his dirty handkerchief until the blood was reduced to only a few droplets on my collar. He sat back on his butt with a gust of relief. "I'm glad tha's over. Ye aren't allowed to get emotional anymore on this trip. Not while I'm the only one here who knows your secret. Bleed all over Bastien, not me. Tha's terrifying."

"I'm sorry, Link. I'm cool now. Tired, though. Thanks for... Have a good night." If Link was embarrassed he'd sung his mom's bedtime song for me, I was equally chagrinned that I'd needed to be sang a lullaby, as if I was a child. I crawled to a spot of grass I hadn't bled on and curled into a ball, hugging myself as I wished for a bed and a little privacy.

Link took the hint, the smarty, and got himself some dinner. He had the decency to eat it near the fire, so I didn't have to hear him slurping on the bacon. I tried not to let my mind wander to Lane, who was probably scared, and trying not to be. We had a way of ignoring the emotions we didn't want to feel until they drifted away. It wasn't working for me tonight, though, but I prayed it was working for her. I could only imagine what hole Morgan had thrown Lane down.

When my mind drifted to Judah, I had to invoke deep yoga breathing to keep myself from crying again. I could picture him in a dark hole somewhere, clinging to the hope that somehow Gandalf would find him. I could practically hear him calling for me, begging me to rescue him. On nights we were scared, we clung to each other in sleep. Judah was afraid of tornadoes, so on the nights it rained without mercy, I would wake to him holding me tight, as if he expected I could make Mother Nature's wrath go away.

Would that I could. I would do anything to give Judah a better life.

When Link settled in behind me inside the ring of dozing horses, I expected him to sit and keep watch. Instead, he lowered himself to the grass. He gave up time he could've been shooting the breeze with the cool kids, and spent it holding me instead. "Ye alright, wee Rose?" he whispered.

"Not really."

"Miss me tha badly, did ye?"

I snorted. "It's the only thing on my mind. I need more Link in my life, for sure."

"Tha's what all the fair lasses say."

"I'm fine. I'm just scared for Judah."

Link was quiet a few beats to be respectful of my very real fear. "So, this Judah fella. He's a good lad?"

"The best Common has to offer."

"And what would he say about a sky like Avalon's?" Link rolled me over so my back was pressed to the grass. He twined his fat fingers through mine, making it feel like we were camping, instead of going on a mission.

"He'd freak out over how many stars there are here. Then he'd start naming all the constellations." I took our joined fingers and aimed both our index fingers at the sky, pointing out a design that was nothing like the stars on earth. "We could call that one fat man on a bucket, because that's what it looks like. I wonder what his story is."

Link chuckled, seeing the design I pointed out. "Maybe he sat down one day to have a good think, and he sat so long that his arse got stuck."

"No way. It's gotta be crazier than that. I mean, Fat Man on a Bucket's got a history, a story to tell. I think he used to be skinny, but he broke his leg when he was trying to learn to dance for the queen. He wanted to be Fred Astaire with a beautiful, talented partner, but no one could keep up. So he danced with a bucket, since no one had footwork fancy enough for him. Then, during his big performance for the queen, he got nervous and tripped over his bucket. He broke his foot, his pride and his dreams of impressing the throne all in one shot. He got so depressed that he locked himself in his home with his bucket, eating himself sick through his misery. He would eat so much that he'd throw up into the bucket. But she never complains, only carries his shame with a quiet grace. On bad days, he yells at his bucket for getting the dance wrong, and ruining his life. But the bucket just sits there, saying nothing, because at the end of the day, she's just a bucket, and nothing more."

Link was quiet as he looked up at the sky. "I don't know why tha story makes me sad."

"I think the sad kind's all I've got tonight, chief." We were quiet, giving me too much time to think. "Link, how come my cuts are already healed from all those ravens attacking, but yours aren't? I mean, my arms look like they never even had a scratch on them."

Link squeezed my fingers, and I could tell he'd been worried about the same thing. "I don't know. Perhaps we don't need to sneeze at the magic tha heals ye, aye?"

"Okay. I was just wondering. Do you think Kerdik really did something bonkers to my genetic makeup? Like, am I different now?"

"Ye look like my Rose to me."

I smirked at his cuteness. "Thanks."

"Will ye sing me one of your Commoner songs? I like those much better than the serious talks about things tha worry me."

I leaned my cheek to his shoulder and smiled sleepily as my eyes closed. "'I see some ladies tonight that should be having my baby.'"

"'Baby.'" Link didn't miss a beat with his line, making us both giggle.

"Goodnight, Link."

He frowned. "Ye didn't say, 'I love ye, Link.' It's not a good night until I know ye love me."

The sweetness that swept over me started at my toes and warmed my entire body, my form curling at the cuteness. "I love you, Link, you old softy."

"I love ye, too. Goodnight, wee Rose."

15

A LOVE FOR THE FIGHT

The next two days were the same, minus the bloody tears. Link had the decency to ask the guys to murder their dinner away from where I slept, so I didn't have to hear the animal suffer and cry for help before the inevitable blow. On the third morning, I expected to wake to Link's goofy antics. He liked to rouse me by blowing a sloppy raspberry into my neck. I'd promised to retaliate by farting on him one of these days, but we both knew I was too chicken to pull that off. Instead, a smooth hand ran down the length of my face, gently lulling me to wakefulness. I rolled over and opened my eyes, blinking a few times before a smile spread over my face. "You! What are you doing here? Dad said you had to go away for a while."

Kerdik gazed down on me with a sweet expression that looked tender and protective. "I did, but I thought I'd pop in for a visit between errands and being banished." He quirked an eyebrow at me. "Did you miss me?"

"Only every day. You alright?"

"Of course I am. Why wouldn't I be?"

I decided there was no time like the present to come clean with my eavesdropping. Link was with the guys a stone's throw away. He was watching me with a cautious expression, and I guessed that Kerdik had made him leave so we could chat. "I sort of overheard your conversation with Brìghde."

A tree nearby suddenly quaked, and then splintered at the base of the trunk before it fell clean over. "No, you didn't. That's not possible."

I sat up and rubbed his arm to soothe his disquiet. "It's alright. You have to stop making trees die when you get upset, though. That can't be good. This place needs more life, not less. We'll have no forest left at all when I tell you I know about the lost magic you gave me, along with my third birth blessing."

I shrieked when a circle of trees sprouted up around us, spooking the horses enough for them to jump up and bolt, so they didn't spontaneously find themselves in a treehouse. Kerdik's eyes never left me, but his smile had deserted our impromptu fort. The trees sprouted branches that twined outwards, winding around each other so we were encased in a circle of Kerdik's making. "Who did Brìghde send to tell you this? How did you find out?"

I could hear the men on the outside shouting frantically. "I'm alright, guys. Link?"

His voice was muffled when it reached me through the foliage. "Rosie, what's going on in there?"

"Nothing. Kerdik doesn't know how to ask for privacy. I'll be out in a few." I stood, arms akimbo as I squared off with Kerdik. "You should really work on that whole temper thing."

"Talk," he demanded, his finger jabbed in my direction.

I kept my voice low, so the others couldn't hear us through the thick tree fort. Their voices were muffled now, the trees keeping our conversation confidential. "I don't know how, but I saw the whole back-and-forth through your eyes. You were super worked up, and I heard it all. I was saying the words you spoke to Brighde, and I heard what your ears did. I saw the same thing your eyes did. For that span of a conversation, I was you. I even felt it when you got worked up."

Kerdik's eyes widened in shock. "That's not possible."

I shrugged. "Neither are bloody tears, but I've got those in spades. That's not a thing that happens in Avalon, then? My magic's gotten so bonkers that it's starting to freak even you out? That's where we're at?"

"It appears so." His eyes were wide as saucers, his fingers covering his mouth. "Are you well?"

"I'm a beast," I said proudly, slapping my bicep. "I killed the Sluagh, in case you were wondering."

Kerdik nodded. "Urien told me. Very impressive. Are you healing alright from the fight?"

"Better than alright," I began, wondering how to ask him what he'd done to me without sounding accusatory. "I got scraped up pretty good when the ravens attacked, but the cuts vanished the next night."

"Is that so?"

I nodded. "Kerdik? Is something..." I bit down on my lower lip, searching for the right words. "Is something wrong with me?"

His voice turned sharp. "Who told you there was anything wrong with you? You're perfect."

His words, much like his love, were always grander than I expected. He held his arms out to me, and I sank into his embrace, making myself at home in his arms for the moment. "What does it mean when you give your blood to someone? What happens to them?"

I could tell Kerdik was debating between the truth and a blatant "Of course Santa's real" type of lie. "It means that I love you very much. I love you enough to protect you, and gamble on Avalon being a better place because you're in it."

"What's happening to me?" I whispered.

He shifted his weight from one foot to the other. "Remember that you were dying. Remember that I gave up my blood to save you. Remember that I love you."

I felt doomed even before the words tumbled out of his

mouth. "Tell me," I demanded, my words muffled in his crisp, white shirt.

"I don't know what's happening to you," he admitted. Beyond something terrible, Kerdik confessing that he didn't know how it all might go down scared me even more. "I know that I healed you, and kept you from death. I know that you cry blood now, but I don't know how to make it stop. Would that I could make all your worries disappear."

"Kerdik, if you know more about what's going on in my body, I need you to tell me. Any details at all would be helpful."

Kerdik lowered his chin, caught in his attempt to omit bits of the truth. "You... your lifespan will be..."

He seemed to be choking on the truth, so I tried to pry it out of him with a guess. "Can I die?"

His eyes turned guilty. "You can't die at the hand of a person or an immortal, other than the Daughters of Avalon. You can die of natural causes, like an animal attack or something. But you already knew that."

I nodded, confirming this information in my mind under the "facts" section. Still, Kerdik looked scared of my reaction, as if he knew more than he was letting on, but was holding back so I didn't tear him a new one. "Kerdik, what aren't you telling me?"

He swallowed hard, finally meeting my eyes with sorrow. "You would have aged beautifully, I'm sure. But after my blood..." He shook his head as he fingered one of my curls. I'd been sleeping in the dirt and traveling without a shower for days, yet he still looked on me as if I was something precious and fragile. I felt like an ox – expected to be useful and rode hard until her last breath, but under Kerdik's gaze I was a ballerina. "You've been granted a second life. You'll have one entire lifespan of an Avalonian – typically eighty years, plus another eighty on top of that. Then you'll pass on."

My mouth dropped open, my brain stuttering as it failed to compute the unreal information. "So I'm going to live to be one hundred sixty years old, but look like I'm twenty-two?"

Kerdik nodded. "Yes, my love. You were inches from death. It was either cut your years impossibly short, or give you double what you were expecting. Given my choices, I think I picked wisely." He studied my shock and concern, his lips pursed as he pushed forward. "It's my turn for the questions, now. When will I get to be with you?"

I shifted my weight from one foot to the other uncertainly. "I hope we're always close. I love you, but I'm with Bastien now."

He stepped forward and lifted my chin so he could look into my eyes. Burning in his heated gaze I saw the passion of a man I couldn't brush off. "Bastien can have you in this life, but when he passes into the mist, I want you to be mine until your last breath." His lips inched closer to mine. "That's as long as my patience can be expected to last."

I stared up at him in shock. "Um, maybe all of this is something you should've told me the second I came to. You should've asked me if a double-long life is what I wanted."

"You were nearly dead! There wasn't exactly time for a conversation."

I pursed my lips, miffed at his very valid point. "Still. I shouldn't have had to accidentally eavesdrop to know what was going on in my own body."

"I wanted you to live your life and make your choices. I didn't want you to choose me because I made the most sense with your lifeline." His lips tightened, but he remained composed. "And you chose him."

"I did." I was unapologetic in my confirmation.

"And you'll choose me when he's dead."

"Jeez! Don't act so sure of yourself. I don't like that you're keeping huge things from me, Kerdik. We're supposed to be friends, which means we're in this together. Stop acting like I'm five, and you have to shield me from the world."

"I don't answer to you," he retorted imperiously, looking down his nose at me with narrowed eyes.

"You do when it concerns my body!"

"I gave you a double portion of life, instead of a quarter of one. You were dying, and I brought you back with enhancements, no less. You'll heal faster, you know. You're welcome. I would've told you eventually."

"When? On my seventieth birthday when I'm looking

like I should still be in college and hanging at the mall?" My hand flew to my mouth. "Oh! If I have kids, they'll look older than me!"

Kerdik rolled his eyes. "I would've probably said something before you hit seventy."

"Oh, you make me crazy. You're being obnoxious."

"And you're being irrational." He paused, and the corner of his mouth lifted. "I love how riled up you get when we fight. When I figure out how to break my curse, we'll find a whole new use for that spark."

I shook my head and motioned between us. "Don't hit on me when I'm tearing you a new one. This isn't sexy."

Kerdik fingered the collar of my shirt with a delicate stroke, and then suddenly jerked me to him. His lips were mere inches from mine, and for a second, my heart vacillated between hitting him and kissing him. I didn't want to feel anything for someone so inherently selfish, but my escalating heartrate betrayed me like a vixen. Kerdik's mouth grazed my malleable lower lip, teasing and silently begging. He wanted me to make the move – to admit to us both that our friendship was more complicated than bowling and beers. All I had to do was kiss the man who was toying with my libido, his arm coiling around my hips and drawing me in so I could feel the scope of his body pressed to mine.

In an act of desperation, I turned my head to the side and pressed my ear to his heart, reminding us both that it was in there. Kerdik wasn't an impassive immortal – he had feelings and desires, just like I did. "Do you love me?" I whispered, unsure if I could be heard above the hullabaloo that was going on outside our fort as the guys started to panic I'd been out of sight for too long.

"Only love, and only you," he replied with the note of a promise. Just like everything else about him, his answer came out a riddle wrapped in poetry. His arm stayed affixed to my lower back, while his other hand lifted mine out to the side, so we could slowly dance together in our secret world.

"Then be good to me. Don't tempt me when I'm trying to be clear about who I am and what I want." I picked my head up to meet his eyes. "I'm with Bastien. If I kissed you now, it would tear me up to step out on a man I truly love. You don't want me stolen. You want me as a gift I give you someday. What you're doing, teasing me like this? You're asking me to be less than I am."

Kerdik's gaze hardened, and his hand stiffened around mine, but he kept up the slow sway he was leading us through. "Stop saying things that keep us apart."

"Brìghde said it'd be just like you to ruin the thing you love. If you steal me from Bastien, that would stamp out one of the things you love about me. You love that I'm loyal. If we do this, that's one less thing to love about me. Compromise after compromise will start to change me from the girl you want into the woman you don't recognize. Then Brìghde will be right. We can't have that."

"I don't like loving you from afar," he admitted, taking

my chastisement with surprising grace. "If you'd never met Bastien, would you consider me then?"

I leaned in and pressed my ear to his chest again. It was my favorite way to hold (and be held by) him. "I don't know. I love you so much, but sometimes you scare me. You're selfish. You could help Avalon in ways no one else can, but you can't be bothered. It's not a real criticism, but being that I'm crossing the country on a horse to save my mom and my Judah, I see the divide between how much I care about a land that's not even mine, and how little you give a crap about the nation you created. I can't imagine we would last as a couple when our focuses are so divided."

He paused before his words came out terse and laced with frustration. "I'll not let you make me feel guilty about letting a world solve its own problems. My solutions often lend more distress than there was before I intervened."

"You made my life better by intervening. You saved me."

"I did save you, and you'll do well to remember that." Kerdik squeezed me tight. "You wish me to help Avalon more?"

I shrugged, thinking my answer through. "No. I want you to be yourself. I'm just saying that you, as you are now, might not be able to make it work with me in the long run. I need someone who cares. Bastien's riding to save my mom, Reyn, Damond, Remy and even Judah, who he barely even knows. He's going in the wrong direction, mind you, but he cares. Not because I told him to care, but because that's who he is. That's how he fights." I pulled back my head and gazed up at Kerdik, studying his handsome features. "You gave up the fight for Avalon a long time ago. You know how much I love a good fight."

Kerdik pondered my words, and then kissed my forehead. "Very well. If you're going to rescue Lane and this Judah boy, then I'll go with you."

I quirked my eyebrow at him as he twirled us in our slow dance. "You're trying to manufacture feelings because I want you to care. I'm not sure that's how it works. Though at this point, I'll take any help I can get. I'm not totally sure what we're walking into."

"Give me time to get there, love. I've got something to tend to, but I'll meet up with you. How far away do you guess they are?"

I looked down at my stomach, checking in with my gut for an answer. "I'm thinking we'll reach them by nightfall."

"I'll find you. Stay safe, sweetheart." He pressed his cheek to mine, making my lashes flutter shut involuntarily. There was something about him that magnetized me to his touch, no matter how much I tried to resist him.

Before I could crumble and admit that I wanted him to stay, he vanished, making me stumble forward as two of the trees toppled over to let me out.

16

FINDING MY JUDAH

When night fell, I knew we were close. I could see flickers of a fire in the distance as we rode with purpose. The guys were still shaken that Kerdik had crashed our party, but as none of them lost their heads in the midst of Kerdik's oft-swinging temper, there was a hushed buzz of energy about them that made me hopeful we might actually win this.

Link led his horse to the right, and slowed to a walk, moving through the trees more stealthily, now that we were close. He held up his fist, and we all came to a stop behind him. "There they are, up ahead. I want ye to draw your swords and be ready for anything. They've stolen the duchess, plus allies to the Avalon Rose, so they get no mercy. Slaughter the lot of them and rescue the prisoners. There's five of them: Duchess Elaine, Judah, Prince Damond, Reyn and Remy, who's Princess Rosie's healer and her knight." His eyes focused in on mine. "We both promised your Da tha ye wouldn't be fighting, so you'll wait here." I opened my mouth to protest, but Link held up his hand with the authority of an Untouchable. He'd gone from goofball to military commander in an afternoon. It was strange to see him in his element. "As soon as we find a prisoner, we'll bring them straight to ye, and you'll guard them here. This is our rallying point."

I nodded, knowing there wasn't a point in challenging his leadership. If I wanted to be treated like a soldier, I had to be able to follow commands. "Yes, sir," I offered with a humble bow of my head. I hoped Kerdik would show up soon.

The men each bowed their heads to me, and I wasn't sure what to do in response. So I blew each of them a kiss, making them smile and rally as they drove their horses to wind stealthily between the trees.

As soon as the men left, Daisy asked if she could go to the stream she could hear running nearby and get a drink. "Sure, baby. I'll wait here, though. I want to be able to see what's going on."

There was an odd absence of animals the nearer we'd come to enemy camp. It was almost as if whatever was going on there was so evil, that even woodland creatures caught the sick vibe.

Judah was there. I mean, I couldn't see him, or anyone, for that matter; I was too far away. But I could see the flickers of firelight way in the distance. My gut screamed at me, telling me that Judah and Lane were in there. I checked for Reyn, and felt his tug, too, but when I checked in on Damond and Remy's whereabouts, the reading came back fuzzy. I could tell they were nearby, but their presence was more nebulous for some odd reason.

I stretched my arms above my head and twisted my waist a few times, waiting to see if I would be able to catch sight of the forthcoming battle. I prayed we outnumbered them, but my heart knew that wasn't Morgan's style. The trap Bastien, Mad and Draper were headed towards certainly was in keeping with Morgan's need for cunning and trickery. Morgan wouldn't send the actual prize away without several failsafes, including a battalion of soldiers so she didn't have to worry about her stolen prize being snatched at.

I really should've been paying closer attention, listening to the clues of no animal life nearby to warn me that something was amiss. The nothing I heard should have alerted me to the fact that a very real something was on the prowl, and headed straight for me.

The dirty hand over my mouth muffled my scream before it got halfway out of me. The breath that wafted over the left side of my face from behind made me want to vomit. "Say a word, and I'll slit your throat right here. If you want to live, you'll shut up and give my boys a good show."

17

CAPTAIN MOSS

$\mathcal{I}$'m not sure I would ever agree to the notion of "going quietly." I writhed and punched and fought with everything in my soul to free myself from the four soldiers who ambushed me. I want to say that I was able to best four grown, armed military men, but that would be wishful thinking.

My spirits rose when my Daisy heard my cries of distress and galloped into the fray. The two of us kicked and pummeled with everything in us, making our marks on the men who would ruin all that was good in the world.

When I heard her whinny of agony, I knew I'd gotten my hopes up too soon. Blood was coating her flank, spilling out onto the grass. She gasped through her pain from too many slices marring her skin.

"Run, Daisy!" I wanted to save at least her, even if I couldn't save myself, but it was too late.

The last sound on my faithful horse's mouth was my name, and it broke what was left of my heart.

They weren't interested in giving me a fighting chance, but rather getting me on the ground as quick as possible. After I landed a solid jab to one dude's throat, another retaliated with a hard wallop across my face. His fist was like granite, whipping my head to the side and knocking me off my game.

Before I knew it, my wrists were bound behind my back with itchy rope, and I was hoisted over one of their burly shoulders. I wanted to summon Kerdik, asking him where the crap he was, but I couldn't put my ring to my chest to call him.

"Haddock, go on ahead and see if you can catch her men en route to the ambush. I'll take the little princess to the post."

"Yes, Captain Moss."

Haddock rode off, ignoring my cries for him to rot in Hell. Captain Moss chuckled darkly as he marched through the woods. "My men will be happy to see such fight. It's been awhile since the duchess lost hers."

Dread coursed through my veins, turning me icy from the inside out. "What have you done to Lane?"

"The queen, may she live forever, told us to keep her and the Commoner alive. Making her wish she was dead? That was a little gift from me for stealing away half of Province I." He marched with purpose, his men trailing behind with two swords drawn apiece. "That she thinks she can take what's ours, what we worked for? The regal queen all the deserters think her to be..." He shook his head and chuckled. "If only they could see her now."

I renewed my struggle, trying to kick at his head and somehow roll myself off his shoulder, but if you can believe it, none of that worked. All it got me was a swift slap to my butt, and then a lecherous grab with a rough massage. My face was red, but I was equally livid as I was horrified at being blatantly toyed with. "Get your perv hands off me, you dick."

I heard swords clashing to my right, deeper in the forest, and knew my guys had found the ambush. I prayed with everything in me that they would be victorious, that they would all come out of this with nothing more than mere papercuts. I was already sporting the beginnings of what I was certain would turn out to be a black eye and some bruises from our scuffle.

Captain Moss kept his brisk pace, taking me in a straight shot toward the fire, where a ten-foot-tall post was erected in the center of the camp. If Kerdik was right about me holding a fair bit of magic from his blood, plus whatever lost magic we had yet to discuss, Captain Moss wouldn't be able to kill me.

I didn't realize how much damage could be done in the space between death and wanting to die.

18

LANE, MY LANE

I was kicking and fighting to no avail the entire way to the camp, unable to see much, other than the Captain's rear end and the grass. When he hefted me off his shoulder and thwacked me on the ground, I bounced twice, he threw me so hard. It took me a few seconds to survey my surroundings in the lanterns' dim illumination, but the first thing I heard in the circle of tents and men's murmurings was Judah's voice cracking above the din. "No! Rosie, run!"

My heart swelled in my chest as my neck craned to locate my bestie. "Judah? Are you…" When my eyes fell on him, a sob choked out of me. "Let him go!" I shouted, as if my command held any weight here.

There was my Judah, his hands tied to a post that was no more than four feet tall. Reyn was with him, tied in the same fashion – a stoic and haunted look to his vacant eyes.

It was as if Reyn didn't recognize me, didn't rally that maybe help was on the way.

At this point, that was a definite maybe.

The only thing that could draw my eyes from the sweetest sight I'd seen in a long time was a moan coming from somewhere behind me. Lane's voice was garbled, but I still knew that sound anywhere. It was the momma bird calling out for her baby. I knew her cadence like I knew the pounding of my own heart. "Lane?" I couldn't turn around to see her yet, because Captain D-bag yanked me up and shoved me toward the tall post, undoing my rope for a few seconds so he could secure the bindings to a hook over-head. It was so tall, I had to stand on my tiptoes.

"That'll do nicely," he said appraisingly, bringing the butt of his dagger under my chin to lift my head. "Fedrir, you brought in the game last night, so you get first crack at the little princess. You know the rules, twenty minutes per customer, and no permanent damage."

I was rage-filled, until Captain Moss stepped away, and my gaze fell on a heap of tanned and naked skin on the ground. I let out a bleat of fear and agony when I took in the face that was bruised and bloody. There was my Lane, my strong and precious mother – without a stitch of clothing on, and beaten so badly all over, I was shocked she could see it was me tied just a few feet from her. "Lane!" I shouted, horrified and scared.

"Rosie?" When her one good eye met mine, dread was visible on her swollen features. "No, no, no, no. Take me instead! Leave my daughter alone. Don't touch her!" She struggled to stand, but only made it to her knees before she trembled and collapsed in the dirt. "I'll play nice! I'll do whatever you want!"

The man I can only assume was Fedrir came up to Lane and roughly grabbed her breast. "You'll already do whatever we want, dog."

"Get your hands off of her!" I shouted, on the brink of losing my mind at my mom being degraded so cruelly.

Fedrir had a missing tooth, a number one branded on his forehead, a bulge in his pants, and a gaze that could turn a girl to ice. He turned to lock eyes with me, letting me know he was in charge, and this was happening. He had to be at least forty. He was old enough to know better, but apparently didn't care. "Is it my birthday or something? Who wrapped up my present?" he joked to the men, who leered as they laughed.

I sneered at him, wondering how the crap I was going to fight my way out of this one. My toes could barely find purchase on the dirt, and my arms were so high over my head, I could barely move. I reminded myself that I was an athlete, not a helpless, scared girl. Well, to be fair, I was both of those things, but I chose to focus on only the one that might get me out of this mess. I could hear Judah shouting obscenities at Fedrir, but couldn't see him anymore. My brain raced, taking in the post as my only tool that might be useful – immoveable as it was. I knew I might only have one shot at this, so I summoned all my courage and strength as Fedrir approached. With a single grunt, I pulled myself up using my biceps, sheer force of will, and the bindings that held me in place. My black boots scraped at the side of the pole in a frantic race to get to the top. I knew I looked like I was trying to climb away from him (if only), but I was just trying to get my ring finger to my heart. My right leg swung out and cracked Fedrir across the mouth, buying me a few extra seconds to regret my choices in life.

But it worked. I managed to heft myself up, press my fist to my heart and whisper, "Kerdik, Kerdik, Kerdik!" before I was yanked back down. Fedrir was pissed now, instead of wanting to entertain the crowd that looked to be about fifty strong. My boots were quickly jerked off my feet by another soldier, along with my socks, and then another man ripped off my jeans. It all happened so fast, I didn't have time to cry. There were five of them around me, knives drawn to make sure I didn't lash out again.

I struggled like a spider being electrocuted, legs flailing and kicking with purpose whenever I could manage the feat. My shirt was torn open by a man who'd never been able to seduce a woman properly, so he felt it was perfectly acceptable to take shortcuts. Then I saw his frustration when he couldn't slide the torn material off my arms. He settled on tying the shirt around the post at my wrists, exposing me under lantern light in my bra and underwear to the men – some of whom were old enough to be my father.

When a flicker of flame brightened my skin, one of the men shouted in surprise. "Captain, she's got the mark of the Untouchable on her! We can't touch her," one of them said, backing up with his hands raised.

Captain Moss sneered, agitated that the gift he'd brought for his men came with fine print. "Anyone who doesn't have a problem breaking the highest law is free to do as he pleases with the princess."

The soldiers looked torn, some falling back and others hesitantly moving forward. A few of them calling out, "I'm not touching, I just want to watch." As if watching the highest law be broken, but not technically breaking it themselves was good enough to service their shred of a conscience.

Fedrir fell back, now that my shirt's collar wasn't hiding my neck tattoo. "I can't, Captain. Someone else have a go. That psychotic Madigan the Formidable must've marked her. I'll not go up against him. If she was just her majesty most high's daughter, that'd be one thing, but I can't break the code of the Untouchable."

Captain Moss harrumphed and barreled through the men to cut off my bra and give my breasts a rough squeeze, as if to show them how it was done. I refused to scream, though the panic welled up like bile in my throat. "See? Nothing's happened to me. I broke the highest law, and I'm still standing. No one had a problem taking their turn with the duchess. A little ink, and now you're all running scared from a sweet little piece like her?" He slapped my butt hard, knocking me against the pole.

I was too terrified to cry, instead vomiting all over the post when a few hesitant and curious men with a death wish grabbed at my exposed body. Lane was screaming as she scrambled to me, but was quickly kicked away by one of the soldiers. The hands multiplied, gaining courage with the Captain's continued assault. I had to get to Lane, to somehow get her out of here.

The vile hands were everywhere, violating and bruising, as if I was the reason they were angry at the world. When my underwear was yanked down my thighs, I head-butted the nearest man, sending him staggering back a few paces. I didn't have a plan, only that I wouldn't go down without a fight. There was too much touching, too many hands. My screams and even my best fight were too ineffectual.

I said a fond farewell to my virginity and my sanity, and gritted my teeth to get though whatever the next phase of my life might be after this unthinkable day.

There was no hope left for any of us.

And then the ground started to shake.

19

MY BRAVE KNIGHT

I thought I'd finally lost my mind when brown vines slithered up the throats of the men surrounding me. There were so many of them now, that I lost count. They couldn't all get close enough to grab at me, but they at least wanted to watch with all the fascination of Superbowl Sunday. One by one, they fell back with choked sounds of surprise, collapsing, and then being dragged away by some invisible force. The hands on me were ripped away, and the sight that greeted me made me finally burst into tears. Red streamed down my face and clouded the green vision of mercy and judgment.

Kerdik and Link ran through the men, who were all choking on the vines that had spontaneously grown from the dirt and grass, and attacked them with vengeance. My heroes charged toward me, faces fraught with distress and fury. Link reached me first, and cut through my bindings with his knife, his teeth gritted in disgust. He didn't stop, but sawed through Lane's bindings next.

Kerdik knelt down behind me and slid my underwear up my body with trembling fingers as the ground quaked with his rage. I brushed the ropes off my unsteady wrists and managed to flip my shirt over my head. My quaking fingers fumbled with the buttonholes that had no buttons anymore, while Kerdik quickly searched for my jeans.

The men choked and writhed on their knees around us, but Kerdik paid their pain no mind. He dressed me with all the respect of a cherished friend, holding me tight when I finally had enough clothes on to feel like a person again. He washed my face without a word, not shushing me or telling me it would all be alright. It was too late for lies like that. The water cleansed my face, but it was the rest of me that felt dirty. "I'm here now, and I'll take care of it," he promised, which turned out to be the only right thing a person could say in that situation.

I didn't understand why Kerdik pulled away from me until I saw him unbuttoning his crisp white shirt and moving toward Lane, who Link was trying to revive with water from his canteen. Lane had been knocked unconscious by the soldier's boot to her face. Kerdik was respectful and somber as he moved to Lane's body. Link was equally careful, turning her this way and that when Kerdik's palms poured out a stream of water to bathe her with.

Lane finally roused, but when her eyes fell on Kerdik,

she gasped in fear that I knew wounded him. Still, he was kind. Kerdik removed his shirt and wrapped it around her, once Link helped her to sit up. They threaded her arms through the shirt, and Kerdik even buttoned her up, keeping his eyes on her scared face the whole time. I could tell he was talking to her, but I couldn't hear anything above the choking and cries for mercy that plagued the air around us.

"Where are the others?" I asked Link.

Link shook his head with a grave expression. "Ambush in the woods. I'm the only one tha escaped."

I held out my hand to Link. "Knife?" I requested when my voice finally found enough strength to be heard.

"Aye. Slit however many throats ye like, love."

I didn't want more violence. I wanted my best friend. I stumbled on rubbery legs over to Reyn and Judah, untying Reyn first, though he didn't seem to see me, and he didn't move once freed. I snapped my fingers in front of his face, but he didn't even blink.

"He's checked out," Judah informed me. "Lost his mind after the first week of them doing all that to Lane. Hasn't said a word in days. Just stares."

I met Judah's eyes, my gaze blazing into his with a promise that somehow I would make this up to him. "I'm so, so sorry. I didn't want you caught up in this." I was clumsy with the knife, trying not to let my fingers slip and accidentally cut him.

"Easy, Ro. It's alright. I think we might be saved now.

Those are the good guys?" he guessed, nodding his head toward Kerdik and Link.

I nodded, biting my lip to keep myself from bawling all over again. When I finally freed Judah, the familiar hug found me, making me ache all over with the love I'd been missing. I didn't care that my torn shirt had fallen partially open, he cared about me. There's something magical and indescribably peaceful about the love of your favorite friend. His grip on me was weakened, but the connection was there. He smelled like the dirt of the ground he'd been confined to, but beneath it was the scent that was inherently Judah. He smelled like the home I'd had to pretend it was fine to live without.

But it wasn't.

"Wait here with Reyn," he instructed after we finally pulled away to get a good look at the difference a year apart had made. He was missing his glasses, but the rest of him was the Judah I loved. "I need to go help Lane."

"Wait. Where are Remy and Damond? There were two other guys who were traveling with Lane. Where are they?"

Judah pointed a dirty finger toward a short post on the far edge of the camp. I hadn't noticed before, but there was a ball or something oblong-shaped atop it. "They killed Damond first and burned his body. Then they tore Remy apart a few days ago. Knocked him around for sport. He was a good guy. Didn't deserve that."

I gasped and let out a horrified scream when I realized

it was Remy's head atop the post. My brave knight, my healer, and my friend – gone without ceremony.

My cousin who'd finally come into his own and left his horrible father – was also utterly destroyed, but without even a trace of him to bring back to Draper. A sob burst out of me, but this was beyond tears.

Remy had sworn his allegiance to me. He'd wanted nothing more than to be my knight. He went with my mom to make sure she was safe on her trek to bring peace to the outskirts of Avalon. Damond had given up his claim on Province 2's throne to build a better world with us. Both their noble efforts came to a violent end that I knew no amount of therapy would ever be able to reconcile.

Judah picked up my hand and put it atop Reyn's. "Wait with him. Lane needs me." I nodded, scooting over to Reyn and wrapping my arms around his neck. Though he was basically a doll with no language or movement, I clung to him to communicate warmth, in case that might help him realize Lane was finally saved.

Remy was dead. Damond was dead. I clung to Reyn's neck tighter to fend off the terror that was just plain too much.

20

DON'T TOUCH MY PRIZE

K erdik came over to me once Link retrieved my pack from the woods, and had given Lane a pair of my pants, underwear and one of my shirts to wear. The fifty men in the camp were still on their knees, drawing in miniscule gasps of breath as they struggled against nature's attack. The vines didn't relent, nor did they put the men out of their misery. They were stuck in their limbo between dead and wanting to die.

Kerdik ignored their strangled pleas and buttoned up his white shirt, along with his gray vest, his fingers no longer trembling. He handed me an untorn shirt from my pack, and then knelt down in front of Reyn, motioning me away from the immobile man. He held out his palm, and I watched a small flower bloom there.

I slid my arms into the welcome garment, startling when a small flame burned the flower to ash. I made a noise of confusion when Kerdik blew the ash into Reyn's face. Reyn didn't even blink, but inhaled the powdery residue as he stared vacantly ahead. His eyes began to grow heavy, and in the next few breaths, he slumped to the ground, unconscious.

"What did you just do?" I asked, unsure how nervous I should be.

"I was merciful. I'm letting Reyn sleep through his pain. He'll wake up when we're back at the palace, and he knows Lane is safe again. I can't imagine if I had to sit through what he's had to witness, if you were on the receiving end of the cruelty. I would beg someone for the kindness of knocking me out." He brushed off his hands and then tucked a lock of hair behind my ear, taking my flinch in stride. "Come with me," he ordered gently, helping me to my feet.

"They killed Remy and Damond. They tortured Remy." I pointed to the post as my stomach roiled. "That's his head."

Kerdik snapped his fingers, and the ground beneath the post sank down into an impromptu hole. Fresh dirt covered Remy's head, burying it so my knight didn't have to look on the horrors of life any longer. He cast around for Remy's body, and dragged it to the same spot, burying the mangled mess in a similar fashion to keep animals from picking at my friend's flesh.

Kerdik returned to my side, his arm coiling around the middle of my back. "I'll not have you plagued by that sight.

He'll not be on display another second." Then Kerdik raised his hand like a conductor, sprouting an oak from nothing, and making it grow into a mature tree, its branches shading the grave of my brave knight who had given up everything for Avalon.

Kerdik walked with me to the trunk, and raised his finger to trace his tight scroll into the bark. "I'm writing your name and Remy's, and then a poem I enjoyed years ago. Is that alright?"

I nodded, the shock still rolling through me. "What does the poem say?"

"It's simple. 'You fought for me, but I never had the chance to win it all for you. I would've fought, my friend, to the very end of ends. Yet there you are, and here I am.'"

I frowned as something pinged in my mind. "That's a song in Common. It's from 'End of Ends', off Lost and Forgotten's second album."

Kerdik shrugged, wondering if I was starting to lose my grip on reality, which I'll admit, wasn't too big a stretch. "Come, darling. Your knight will rest now. Where is Damond's body? Help me find your cousin."

"Burned," I croaked with a grimace. "Thank you." I clung to Kerdik as we walked toward the center of the camp, stepping around the red-faced men who were still writhing on their knees. Kerdik stroked my cheek and held me close. We walked in-step, as if we were one body.

Judah was kneeling with Lane, who was rocking herself in the dirt, clinging to the clothes on her bruised body as Judah held her together. I could tell it was the first loving touch she'd had in too long, because she gripped Judah tightly while she sobbed.

"It's over, now. It's all over," Judah whispered, squeezing her tight with tears streaming down his cheeks. He didn't have his glasses on, and the only mercy in all of it was that hopefully Judah hadn't been able to see every detail of the horror his surrogate mother had been forced to endure.

Link's voice boomed out across the camp. "Which of ye are guilty of breaking the highest law?" He was livid, his sneer in full swing as he paced with his sword drawn. "Rosie's marked as ours. She belongs to the Brotherhood. She belongs to Madigan, to Bastien, to Nicholai, to Antonio, and to me. Which of ye touched my prize?" He sounded like a furious child, barking at a schoolmate who'd snatched at his toy.

When no one fessed up (I mean, I'm not totally sure what sort of honesty Link was expecting from a bunch of murdering rapists), Link turned his furious gaze in my direction. "Which of them, Rosie? Whose hands touched my prize?"

I was mute with stage fright, unsure what I should do. I didn't want violence to be solved with more violence, but I couldn't let the men go free after all they'd done; they'd just find another woman to terrorize. "I... I don't know."

Link moved to the nearest man, bunching his hand in tufts of the dude's hair and yanking upward as far as the vine could stretch, exposing the guy's Adam's apple to me.

"What of this bloke? Did he touch my prize?" Spittle flew out from Link's mouth, and all of his muscles were tensed in preparation for the blow.

Lane's voice cracked above the din. "Yes! He broke the highest law, Link. He touched Rosie."

Link nodded, as if he'd been hoping for this answer. In a move so swift, I couldn't look away in time, Link sliced clean across the man's throat, spilling blood all over the front of his red and gold uniform. I yelped and hid my face in Kerdik's shirt, not wanting to see such a gruesome scene.

I was surprised when Kerdik turned my chin to face Link. "No, darling. You'll not close your eyes through this. You'll see every one of your attackers put to death, so you don't lose a single night's sleep, thinking they might come for you."

"I don't want to see this!"

Kerdik held my face so that I didn't miss a second of the violence. "This is a kindness Link is paying you. Watch him, so you know you're safe with the Untouchables. Seeing them defend their territory?" He shook his head in admiration. "You don't get warriors this pure anymore."

Link moved to the next soldier, yanking his hair up in the same way. "How about this one, sweetheart? Did he touch my prize?"

I was still dumbstruck, too scared to speak out in my own defense. Judah saw me freezing up and shouted, "They all did! They all deserve to die."

I couldn't believe such vile words birthed from Judah's

mouth. I didn't blame him, but still. It was a shocker. Avalon had that effect on people, I guess.

Link nodded, as if waiting to hear this exact answer. Still, as he moved through the camp, he incited more and more fear in the remaining soldiers when he shouted out with a booming brogue, "What of this lad? Did he touch my prize?" as he approached each one, putting him on display for me. Kerdik held me, and Judah held Lane as one by one, all the men fell at Link's capable sword. His vengeance was controlled, which was the most terrifying thing about it. Anyone can go on a blind rage, but to stalk your prey, put them on display, read out their sentence and carefully select the next victim struck a spine-tingling fear in the remaining soldiers.

Bloody tears streaked down my face, mercifully clouding my vision by blinding me. It was a kindness my new genetics paid me, and for once, I didn't resent the crimson that stained my cheeks. I was grateful that I didn't have to see the rest of the men bleeding out on the dirt at Link's feet.

21

HOME SWEET HOME

Kerdik's hand didn't leave me the entire way home, staying affixed to my spine as if to assure me that all men weren't disgusting, and that all touch wasn't bad. Judah did the same for Lane, since Reyn was still unconscious. When we reached the castle, everyone was careful with the rescued prisoners. Link helped Judah down from the horse as if Judah was a little boy, though I knew anything youthful in Judah had most likely been stamped out by now, courtesy of Avalon.

I let Kerdik carry me inside. We both knew I could walk just fine, but Kerdik needed to show me that men could be kind. I needed to let him teach me that lesson, lest I forget it forever.

Link was gentle with Lane's form as he carried her into the castle. She looked so fragile and broken that we were all afraid she might not make it back alive. "I need a healer!" Link bellowed as he entered our home. The servants yelped at the state of their duchess and ran to fetch Jean-Luc and my father.

My dad reached us first, crying out in fear when his eyes fell on us. "Lane? No! What did they do to you?" Link surrendered Lane to my dad, whose eyes welled as he carried her up to her bedroom.

Jean-Luc was summoned to examine Reyn and Lane in her chambers, and a second healer I'd met in passing once was called to examine Judah and me. Judah was physically alright, with only a few bruises and bumps, but the haunted look in his eyes was the thing that worried me most. How many horrors had he been given a front row seat to? How many world-shattering crimes had he been forced to witness?

Our healer's name was Pierre, and he did Judah a kindness by giving him a potion to knock him out, so he could sleep through the night. I wondered how Judah would ever find rest again that was not chemically induced. As my bestie's eyelids drooped and rose, drooped and rose, he laid on my pillow as he'd done in Common almost every night in the past however many years. It was an odd thing to see Judah be at home in my world, but part of my heart felt healed at having him around again. Kerdik was sitting in a chair in the corner of my room, watching quietly as I fawned over Judah, fluffing his pillow and brushing his dark, curly hair away from his forehead.

"Ro?" Judah said quietly, fighting the sleep that was creeping up to claim him.

"Yeah, Judah? What do you need? What can I get you?"

"Just be here when I wake up, okay? You were right to send me away when you had to go to Avalon. This place is a hole. I was mad at you for a while, but I get it now."

I leaned over and wrapped my arms around him, relishing the feel of my best friend. "I'm so sorry you were dragged into this. I love you so much. I don't want this for you."

"Ro?"

I tucked the comforter under his chin. "What can I do for you? Anything at all, you name it."

Judah's eyes were closed when he murmured, "I missed you, Hot Mama."

I barked out a surprised laugh that Judah had the wherewithal to joke around in a situation like this. "Goodnight, Pimp Daddy." I bent over his body and rested my head on his chest, grateful he was alive, and that somehow he'd managed to keep his quirky sense of humor when Avalon was intent on stamping out the good parts in the very best of people.

22

KERDIK'S HELP

I released Judah when I was certain he was asleep. I felt Kerdik's intense gaze on me, and turned to offer him a tired smile. Our horse had exhausted me on the way home, asking me every other minute if I was alright, the sweetie.

"Let's get you clean." Kerdik stood from his chair and moved behind the partition to fill my tub for me. Though I didn't want to be parted from my clothes, I was filthy, and wanted to wash the molesting hands off of me. "Do you want help?" he offered when my hands slipped on my buttons.

I cast him what I hoped looked enough like a smile to pass as the real thing. "I think I've got this. Thanks, though. After I get in, you can come on back, if you want."

He pressed his lips to mine in a closed-mouth gesture of sweetness. "I always want." He waited until I was submerged to rejoin me, sitting on the floor next to the tub so we could be together. I shifted slowly in the water as I washed myself, listening to him talk about how Avalon used to be. "That sort of thing would never have happened. Urien had a hold of his men, and their only resounding cry was whatever he commanded. He was beloved because he was a decent man. A noble soul brings out the goodness in others. Morgan stamped out Urien, then took the army and twisted it, so that it's unrecognizable now. Urien used to train with his men, letting himself be bossed by the captain, so the soldiers could see that he trusted the commander implicitly. The men fought that much harder to keep their king and his land safe."

"That's really beautiful. I wonder when it all changed."

"Slowly over the years after Urien was put into his deep sleep. It all broke loose when Morgan doused a selection of her soldiers with the acid that made them rabid to obey her. Gave them extra strength and whatnot."

I nodded, remembering the old Popeye dude that had started this whole mess way back when I'd lived in Common. "Super strength plus will control. Not sure how she pulled that one off."

Kerdik and I shot the breeze, talking about how things used to be, and how he wished they were, admitting that was part of why he stayed away for so long. "When Urien was gone in his slumber, the land shifted. There was nothing for me to come back to, no one left I wanted to stay for." His forearm draped over the lip of my tub, making himself at home in our very private moment. "Let me wash your back."

My cheeks heated as I shook my head. The rose-ish smell of the petals he'd brewed my bath with were luscious and fragrant. The sun had set, so the flickering candles were the only light in the room, aside from the blue hue of the moon. "I don't think that's a good idea. You being back here behind the partition with me probably isn't a good idea, come to think of it."

"And yet, here I am." He gazed into my eyes, and the only sound was the gentle lapping of the water as I shifted the soap around to wash my own back.

I chewed on my lower lip. "I used to have a hump, you know. Big time scoliosis."

"I can't imagine that."

"Every time you look at me like I'm something special, I wonder if you would've given me the time of day back when I had no boobs, a hump, a lazy eye, and a face full of acne."

"You're the loveliest woman I've known, that's for certain, but it was your spirit that sucked me in that first time we met. You were more concerned for my safety than you were for your own, and I was a mere stranger. Always their princess; always my queen." Kerdik took a chance and dipped his fingers into the water to warm it for me, making me hmm contentedly. "Lane was prudent to hide your beauty, even though she didn't know about the third birth blessing. Your sweet soul would have made you the loveliest woman in all of Common."

"Prudent, yes. It was hard to grow up looking like that, though. So when men stare at me like I'm something to look at, I don't know how to handle that kind of attention. I didn't realize the downside of looking like this would be that some men would think they could just take me, like how the soldiers did." I clenched my knees together under the water, and drew them to my chest. "I miss my hump and not having boobs. Guys left me alone in Common. I was the dude friend, and didn't have problems like this."

Kerdik reached through the water and found my hand, clasping my palm as if we were readying to arm-wrestle. "I adore you," he whispered like a promise. "In whatever stage your body finally comes to me in, that will be the one I cherish. If I hadn't given you my blood, and you were to age, my fetish would be white hair and wrinkles. Whatever you are, that's what I love."

My eyes misted over with the blinding red that turned a precious moment into something that spooked me. My movements became jerky in the tub when I couldn't see anything. A whine of distress came over me until Kerdik's thumbs washed the red away. When I opened my eyes, I only saw green. Kerdik's face was close enough to kiss, and for a moment, I wanted to give in to the desire that never seemed to subside. I resisted, leaning my forehead to his so I could take in a few steadying breaths. "You can't say beautiful things to me. I want to hear them too badly."

He gripped the edge of the tub, and for a second, I thought he might tear his clothes off and climb in with me. He hesitated, and then sat back on his heels, giving us some much-needed space. "I need to wait out there for you. I'm afraid if I see you in the tub a moment longer, I'll turn you into a dragon this very night."

My eyes widened, but I said nothing as he stood and moved to the other side of the partition. I finished washing myself, and then tucked the thick towel around my body, tiptoeing out to find something to wear. Kerdik handed me one of Bastien's flannels from our wardrobe, and I quirked my eyebrow at him. "Hello, you really want me to wear this? You threw a fit last time you saw me in it."

"You belong to Bastien for now. Seeing you in his clothes will keep me from seducing yours off your creamy shoulders. I would have loved you in your Commoner state, but that you've come to me in such a succulent package? Immortal that I am, you forget that I'm a man. I'm not above temptation." He held the shirt open for me to shove my arms through, and then turned me around so he could button me up over my towel. The terrycloth came free in a shake, and pooled at my feet on the floor. Kerdik shut his eyes in pain and took a step back. "Yes, that'll do it." He moved to the chair in the corner of the room and sat down in it, covering his face with his hands to exhale his exasperation into his palms.

Though he didn't ever have thirst, being who he was, I poured him a cup of juice from the pitcher that had been brought in for me on my picked-over dinner tray. "Here, you look like you've had a long day." I handed him the cup and moved over to the bed, making sure Judah hadn't stirred, or kicked his covers off. I watched his chest rise and fall, reassuring myself that my bestie was okay. We had each other again, so somehow it would all be alright. "I need to go check on Lane, but I'm afraid if I leave Judah, he'll be scared if he wakes up and I'm not here." I kept my eyes from Kerdik. "C-could you help me write him a note?" I hated asking for help with something a second-grader could do. I shook my head, embarrassed and ashamed. "Never mind. I'll just stay here."

Kerdik stood and grabbed a quill and some parchment from a desk in the corner I'd never fully investigated. "After all we've been through, I can't understand why you're still hesitant to ask me for help with the simplest things."

"It's a huge hit to my self-esteem to admit to someone as powerful as you that I can't do something any dummy can."

Kerdik scribbled something on the page, and then read it to me. "Dear Judah, I'm in the northern corridor on the seventh floor in Lane's chambers. I'll be back soon, so don't leave the room."

"Can you cross out Judah and write 'Pimp Daddy'? Then he'll know it's me who wrote it."

Kerdik quirked his eyebrow at me, but complied. "Alright, done. Did you want to sign your name?"

I took the quill and haphazardly scribbled my off-kilter signature that was completely illegible, and bore no resemblance to my name, or any actual letters. The signature looked pretty to me, though, almost like a series of diamonds and loops with a squiggle on top.

Kerdik frowned down at it. "Well, he's not going to know it's you." He quickly scrolled my name in no doubt perfect calligraphy. Judah would make a font out of Kerdik's handwriting, and I'd be stuck in the back of the class with my head down, praying the teacher didn't call on me.

I moved over to the wardrobe and slid on a pair of clean jeans, smirking when Kerdik held his elbow out to me, like a gentleman. He led me through the castle slowly, steering me around cracks in the floor where the stones didn't meet. I felt like a lady, which was an incredible difference from how I'd been treated by the soldiers, and how I'd spent most of my life in Common. It dawned on me that Kerdik was learning to love – to give the affection he felt, rather than just be consumed by it. I stopped our progression and turned to stare up at him in the empty stone hallway that was lit only by the flame in his palm. "What's wrong, darling?"

I didn't respond right away, but lifted myself onto my tiptoes and looped my arms around his neck. I was worried I would say the wrong thing, so I was quiet for a few beats, choosing my words carefully. "You saved me," I whispered in his ear. "Thank you. I don't know what I would've done."

His palm cupped the back of my head, holding me close so that our chests expanded together, and we breathed the same breath. "If I hadn't saved you, I don't know what *I* would've done."

We walked in-step, his arm around me, and my hand on his chest as I was tucked tight to his side. Though I understood fully why people saw Kerdik as a monster, he was *my* monster, who treated me like a person when I felt like garbage. It's a good man who can make you feel like a treasure when you're certain you're trash.

He led me the rest of the way to Lane's room slowly, opening the door when the guard posted outside fell away without question. Kerdik was the infinite key to any door. He kept his arm around me as we walked in together to the sounds of quiet sobbing.

There was my Lane, still sporting a few fading bruises and too many cuts peppering her arms and face. She was wearing a sweater and a pair of Reyn's pajama pants that swallowed her form. She was clinging to a damp, white handkerchief and crying with a quiet dignity in the safety of my father's arms. I always forgot that they were brother and sister by law. To see her lean on anyone was a sight for sore eyes. She had lived such a difficult life, and had to bear much of that pain by herself.

My dad was tender to her, motioning us forward to let us know we were welcome to share in her suffering. My dad's arms were strong and safe, and that's what Lane needed right now. My heart ached, and though I wanted to turn away from the sight that was my best girlfriend in such pain, I dropped Kerdik's embrace and ran to her, climbing into the bed so I could wrap my arms around my mom.

"I killed Avril," Lane admitted in lieu of a greeting. It seemed as if her mind was skipping, picking off-topic thoughts that spewed out of her at random. "I wrote it in a note to send home to you, but it never made it here. I said that I loved you." Her voice caught as she began sobbing. "I told you that I would get Avalon back on track, so that we could go back home and have our life. I miss us!"

"I miss us, too!" I admitted, doing my best not to tear up. I truly did long for nothing more than our simple life. The dance routines we made up to our favorite Spice Girls songs, the weird cookie recipe experiments, the road trips to unimpressive places that still managed to wow us because we were together. I missed it all.

Lane's eyes were wet and ringed in red. Her nose was puffy, and I wondered how long she'd been crying. "I killed Avril for what she did to Avalon. I didn't want it to come to that, but she's dangerous!"

Urien held her tighter, nonplussed at her revelation. It looked like Lane had already told him this, and the confession now was for my benefit. "Avril had her fun. I know she stole the Jewels of Good Fortune from you and Roland for her own advantage, at the expense of the people who desperately needed their blessings. You killed her and took her jewel so you could provide for her people, who have already begun to come to our borders."

"I can't believe Reyn kept the gem hidden the whole time from those awful soldiers," Lane hiccupped. "I shouldn't have done it! I murdered my own sister! Who does that? I'm a horrible person!"

Urien shook his head. "No. You are a duchess who protects her people. Avril's subjects are welcome here. There is no room for gray when it comes to protecting our people. Avril is either for us or against us. There cannot be mercy for the wicked when the safety of hundreds of thousands rests on our shoulders. You did the right thing."

"The right thing doesn't feel like this!" she protested.

Urien's voice quieted. "The right thing must be done, no matter what it feels like. Avril did not represent Avalon as she should have. Her people are saved from her heavy taxes and from fear of her waging war on neighboring lands for more gain. They're safe now. You did that for them."

As soon as I made contact, Lane's demure tears turned into howls of agony. I did my best to hold her together, but she was utterly broken. "This isn't where your adventure ends," I assured her as best I could. "Avril is not your adventure, and neither is Avalon."

Lane bawled without chagrin. "I was so scared for you! You should never have come to find us! They almost... And then they... My baby!" She turned in my father's embrace and threw her thinned arms around me, pulling me closer so she could make sure I was real.

"What did they do to you? What happened?"

Lane and Urien both shook their heads. "You can guess enough of what happened," Lane explained. "I don't want you to live with the details. It was awful and painful and scary, but I'm safe now." She motioned to Kerdik, who was standing a socially safe distance from the bed. "You," she breathed, dabbing at her face. It took some doing, but she managed to stumble out of the bed on unsteady legs, and then lowered herself to kneel at Kerdik's feet. It was the strangest sight I'd seen in ages, and I couldn't stop myself from gaping at my mom. Lane kept her chin tucked to her chest, humbling herself to the point of even making Kerdik uncomfortable. Her voice came out tremulous, but certain. "You saved us. You saved my daughter. I owe you my life for what you spared my Rosie. Thank you, Master Kerdik. Thank you."

The sight of my mom on her knees before my... whatever Kerdik was to me was so unnatural that I couldn't look away. Even stranger was when Kerdik lowered his head and placed his hand on her freshly washed hair. "Always know that if I am here, your daughter will be safe."

Lane let out a sob of relief as she butted the crown of her head to his knee. "Thank you."

It was too much for me, my hand over my mouth and worry on my face that this was what life had done to my Lane. Kerdik seemed to sense my disquiet, so he offered his hand to my mother, helping her to stand before him. He shot her several unsure glances before opening up his arms to her. "May I?"

Though it wasn't the gust of relief I usually crashed into him with, Lane slowly let herself get swallowed by the respectful hug he offered. Her voice came out pinched, on the verge of more tears. "I don't know everything in life, but I know that the man who puts clothes on my daughter and on me is someone this world can't survive without. I needed your magic out there, but I also needed someone to be kind and clothe me. You... You were... And then you..." Her composure broke as she blubbered on his shoulder. "I didn't want anyone to see me like that!"

Kerdik's palm gently moved up and down her back as he shushed her. "I didn't see a thing, and neither did Link. Your daughter is safe, and no one will lay a hand on you in my presence." He tucked his finger under her chin so she had to look up at him through damp lashes. "Say, 'I trust you, Master Kerdik.'"

"I trust you, Master Kerdik."

"Good. Now, back into bed with you. You've been through enough, and shouldn't trouble yourself with formalities like bowing and gratitude." Kerdik led her back to the bed with Urien and tucked the covers over her lap, unsure of himself for maybe the first time. I expected something asinine to tumble out of his mouth, but he pushed out a humble, "Are you going to heal?"

Lane let out a nervous laugh. "I think so. Physically, at least."

"I can knock you out so you can sleep, if you need. Reyn's still out from his dose."

"And thank you for that. Reyn wasn't... It's something no man should watch his fiancée have to go through. That was a kindness, and I won't forget it. But I'll need to get back to the people, let them see that I'm home and well. As soon as my face isn't like this, I'll need to be on my feet again."

Kerdik didn't argue, though I wanted to. "As you wish it. I knew it would take more than a battalion of soldiers to break you. You were always the only Daughter of Avalon I had faith in. Your sisters were all either cruel or weak. You have always been strong and kind. Never forget that. Those soldiers could never take something like that away from someone like you." Kerdik stepped back, and let me take the space on Lane's other side in the bed. I didn't waste a second cozying up to her. Just being near me seemed to calm her down.

Lane hiccupped into my hair. "I was wrong about you. I still think you're dangerous, but you're no danger to Rosie anymore. That you would rescue us like that? That you'd dress my daughter when she'd been so carelessly handled? Thank you."

Kerdik's jaw tightened, not used to being complimented so sincerely. "I'm in love with Rosie," he suddenly declared. My jaw tightened, but I didn't tell him to shut up.

He was making himself emotionally vulnerable, and I couldn't bring myself to stifle the inch of growth.

Urien stiffened, but Lane nodded. "I figured as much. Part of me wants to send you away, but the other part of me wants to tell you that I'm happy something so wonderful finally opened your heart. Good for you, Master Kerdik."

"Thank you."

"Rosie chooses her own path, though, and whatever she wants, you'll have to accept."

Kerdik lowered his chin. Their roles suddenly switched from him having all the power, to now Lane holding the cards. "Yes, ma'am."

Lane kissed my nose, suddenly gasping at the sight of my face. She had been knocked out for much of the ride home – another kindness of Kerdik. He'd used more of the powder on Reyn, though, so he was still out. "Your eye. Why's your left eye different? And your skin. I mean, you're gorgeous, but you look almost peachy, like you're glowing or something. Are my eyes going bonkers?"

I shook my head. "You don't need to worry about that right now."

Kerdik spoke up, taking control of the conversation. "You should know that she was injured while you were gone. She was attacked by too many peludas, and was horribly disfigured. She was a few breaths from dying, so I gave her my blood."

I winced at the admission I hadn't seen coming. "I don't think she needs to worry about all that right now, K."

Kerdik ignored me. "I've never done that before, so I didn't know what would happen for sure. Brìghde did it once to save her husband, but each immortal is different. Rosie survived, but there are changes. She and I are connected now. She can see through my eyes when I'm upset." He cast a worried glimpse at me. "She can tell if I lie. Her eyes are different now, but one of the drawbacks is that her tears have turned to blood." He pinched the bridge of his nose. "It's quite disorienting for her, so try not to let her get worked up if I'm out. The tears blind her, and she gets frightened when she can't see."

Lane confined her reaction to a few loud gasps. "You cry blood now? Baby, that's awful! Are you alright?"

I snuggled into her arms, holding her every bit as tightly as she held me. "That you can care about anyone else right now is beyond me, after all you've been through. You're such a good mom. I'm fine. I'm alive. It's a good excuse not to let myself be such a cry baby."

Kerdik wasn't finished, though I wished he was. He explained to my dad and to Lane about my extended life-span, much to their cries of shock and upset. I kinda wished I wasn't there for that part. Kerdik laid everything out on the table, making me itch to run from the room. I kissed Lane's forehead and my dad's cheek, and then made some lame excuse about checking on Judah so I could bolt. I didn't know who I was going to be in fifty years, and didn't want Kerdik planning it all out for me.

23

ALL I WISH FOR

I tiptoed through the hallway, opening my door and peeking at Judah, who was still asleep. Gingerly, I climbed into the bed with him, making sure my movements didn't rock him to wakefulness. I laid down on his left – a.k.a. my spot, and placed my hand in his, how we used to do. Judah's hands were meant for typing and designing on computers. His fingers were long and thin, uncalloused and responsive to my touch. Though he didn't open his eyes, he murmured my name in his sleep. "I'm here," I promised, squeezing his hand. "Go back to sleep."

I don't know why I couldn't get the feeling of the greedy hands of the soldiers off my body, but they were all over, reading my curves as if they were stamped with Braille. I'd been naked in front of all those strangers, tied to a pole like an animal and left completely vulnerable. I shut my eyes and tried not to picture the scene that made vomit churn in my gut. I wanted to put it all behind me in a fit of "Who cares? Nothing affects me. I'm awesome," but I couldn't fake that much confidence this late at night. The horses had spent much time consoling me on the way home, tiring me, but not enough to where I could push the men's hands out of my mind completely.

Not ten minutes later, Kerdik slipped into my room. I sat up to whisper a greeting, but he frowned at me and moved to go sit in the chair he preferred, which was off in the corner of my room. Kerdik crooked his finger at me, beckoning me to leave the bed and go to him. When I neared, he parted his thighs and slowly pulled me down to sit on his lap. Tipping me back and looping my knees over the arm of the chair, he situated my body so I could be cradled in his arms, like a baby. "You'll sleep right here tonight. I'm afraid I can't stomach putting you into bed with another man. I have to share you with Bastien, but I don't know this boy."

I was too exhausted to argue. I knew Kerdik couldn't be dissuaded when he was being stubborn. "Judah's cool." I situated myself in his arms, knowing that nothing could get at me if he was near. "Hey, Kerdik?"

"Yes, darling?"

"Thanks for coming when I called. I like to think I can handle myself in a fight, but I didn't have a prayer. If you hadn't shown up..." I gulped, and clutched his shirt, as if the fabric might keep the feeling of the filthy hands on me away.

"But I did. I told you, I'll never hesitate again to come when you call. I want you to count on me, to call again whenever you need anything. To see your beautiful body tied up like that?" Kerdik closed his eyes in pain. "Even over the smallest thing, call me. Stop trying to tough it out. You should've summoned me the second the soldiers took you."

"Everyone uses you," I explained, my cheek on his shoulder. "I don't want you to confuse me with everyone else. That's why you hated the Daughters of Avalon, because they only called you when they needed help. I don't want you to resent me like that. There's only so much anyone can assist an immortal who's as powerful as you are; I'm already on unequal footing with you, just because I'm a regular person, and you're you. Besides all that, I don't like to parade around the fact that I sometimes need help."

"Do you really not see how much I've grown since I met you? I couldn't resent you for needing my magic if I tried. You're welcome to take what you need from me, whenever you wish. You can have all of me, Rosie. I so very badly wish you would."

"This is all I wish for right now," I replied simply, cuddling into his arms. I also wanted Bastien home, but I didn't think that was quite the right thing to say in the moment.

Kerdik's voice was quiet, speaking low into my ear. "You

wished for me to care about something that wasn't you, right?"

I yawned. "That would be nice, yes. To see you fight for good things in the world is something a girl likes to see."

He clutched me and buried his nose in my hair. He inhaled the scent as if it was more precious to him than any flower he could command to bloom with a wave of his hand. "I always knew Morgan's soldiers had grown depraved, but until I saw you caught up in their wicked games, I didn't care much. It wasn't my problem. Morgan is who she is, and I've learned long ago that I can't change people. But after seeing you tied like that? I think I've found the thing I want to be passionate about."

"Is that so? That's good to hear, K." I yawned. "Tell me all about it."

"I want to help Lane make her province stronger, once she's back on her feet. Normally I don't like to get involved, but I think I might regret not lending a hand. When Morgan comes for you again, I don't want anything to be able to snatch at you. If you say it's not our time to be together, I can accept that, but I won't leave you unprotected, just because you're not mine yet."

I snuggled into his warmth. People assumed Kerdik was cold, but I knew better. His heart could be big, and he'd had to work hard to ignore his baser urges. "I don't deserve you."

"Oh, my love. Don't you know what a wretched man I

am? I would burn this whole nation to ash if you asked me to."

"Let's save the fireworks as a solid plan B." I nuzzled my nose to his cheek, and finally lost the battle with my drooping eyelids. "I love you, Kerdik."

He squeezed me, and his eyes shut, as if he was in pain. "How I do love you, my darling."

"Goodnight," I murmured as I drifted off to sleep in his arms.

24

MY WARRIOR

I awoke in the middle of the night to sounds of shouting down the hall. "Rosie? Rosie!" jerked me awake seconds before my bedroom door burst open. The sight that greeted me made my heart ache. Bastien was disheveled, and looked like he hadn't bathed in days. His flannel shirt was untucked, and his boots were muddy. Still, he took my breath away. "Rosie?" He crooned my name with a palpable anguish – tender and still fraught with distress.

I lifted my head from Kerdik's shoulder and tried to smile for my warrior. Kerdik stood from his chair, lifting me and carrying me toward Bastien. Though my legs were fully capable of walking, my feet never touched the floor. It was as if Kerdik sensed I'd suffered too much to have to deal with such arduous tasks as walking.

With controlled disappointment, he carefully handed

me over to Bastien, giving him the warning of, "Gentle, now. She was attacked, and barely made it out intact."

Bastien nodded, his eyes locking in on Kerdik's with a solemn nod as he sat in a chair with me cradled in his arms. "Attacked how?"

"Morgan's soldiers took her clothes and tied her to a pole. Tried to take what wasn't theirs." Bastien let out a bleat of agony as Kerdik explained with clinical accuracy the whole thing, including the blip of me being able to see through his eyes when he got worked up. It was a long conversation, with plenty of interruptions from Bastien's confusion, outrage, and eventually his heartbreak. Each time he tried to comfort me, Kerdik redirected him, making sure the whole story was told.

When Kerdik explained my extended lifeline, Bastien paled. "So we won't grow old together," he stated, his tone flat.

Kerdik's eyes drifted to the ceiling as he practiced reining in his words. "She'll stay with you until your last breath, no doubt. I'll never understand the loyalty she feels for you, even without her *lueur* inside of you."

Bastien clutched me tight, and though I wanted to tell him I could stand on my own, I was grateful he hadn't dropped me when one hurdle after another came at him. "Okay, then. I've got it from here." There was a distinct but not totally rude "get out" to Bastien's tone.

Though Kerdik wasn't one for being bossed around, I'm sure he didn't want to be here for our reunion. "I'll see you in the morning. If you need me, I'll be with Urien, helping take care of Lane."

My heart tugged in my chest that he would look after my mother for me. Lane was my treasure. That he understood it all and guarded my pot of purest gold when I couldn't? It was a testament to how sincere his transformation from selfish dude to actual grown man had become. I didn't know what would happen in fifty years; I only knew that tonight I was grateful for all that Kerdik was to me, even if we didn't have the words to define it all just yet.

25

THUG LIFE

It was a long night of catching Bastien up on everything until I finally fell asleep in his arms. When morning came, he hadn't moved from the spot on the floor where he'd sunk down to hold me tight through the night. He wasn't too keen on putting me in a bed with Judah, either. I didn't want to admit how shaken I still was, or how much I needed him to stay with me, and never ever leave. In the morning, he talked to me through the partition the entire time I bathed just to quell my nerves. Even as Bastien dressed after his bath, the partition that separated us was too large a divide. "It was a bad idea for us to split up," I whispered, trying not to wake Judah.

"Agreed. It's what Morgan wanted, though. She almost seemed pleased to see us without you. I don't get it."

I shrugged. "What's to get? Morgan's crazy. Did she hurt you guys?"

"Not a scratch. She knows she can't touch me or Mad. She didn't go after Draper, either. Just sent us on stupid time-wasting missions to try and earn Lane back. 'Bring me a fruit from the tallest tree in Province 1, and you can have one of the prisoners.' Then when we did, she'd give us some random prisoner and laugh. Mad lost his patience and went on a tear, slaughtering dozens of soldiers and throwing their bodies on her dais. Then he barged into the castle, and that's when we saw that Lane and them weren't in the dungeon at all. She sent us running around like little chumps just to amuse herself and waste our time. I can't stand that woman." He came out from behind the partition with a clean flannel on and a pair of jeans. "What?" he said of my loving stare. He looked down at his clothes, making sure he hadn't put his shirt on backwards or something.

"I love the look of you freshly clean. I like the look of you in my home."

Despite all he'd been through, Bastien cast me a smile. "Actually, I'm in your bedroom. *Our* bedroom, really."

"Well, you look pretty spectacular here, too." I leaned up on my toes and kissed him, sighing into the connection that helped erase the hands that felt seared on my body. "Tell me we're safe now."

"If I'm here, you're safe," he vowed as his arms wrapped around me. I'd missed the familiar feel of his bulk, and leaned in for another kiss, and another. My *lueur* rose up in me, the little matchmaker, eager to return to Bastien. There wasn't the whole song and dance of a painful transition this time, but merely a shared gasp before he slid the tip of his tongue across mine. "That's better," he murmured contentedly.

My hand reached between us and touched his chest, feeling the heat that settled there. We kissed again and again, relishing the reunion that was peaceful after so much turmoil had rocked our respective boats. "Show me where you're hurt," I whispered, running my hands over his biceps.

"Morgan can't touch us. I'm not hurt. A little sore from riding a horse for days, but nothing more than that." His eyes flicked to my body. "Do you want to wear one of my flannels?" he suggested, knowing better than to ask if I was hurt. The pain I felt went deeper than my faded black eye, which was mostly yellow now.

I nodded, crossing my arms over my breasts. Men putting their hands on me hadn't been a problem when I'd had my hump. Though Bastien's shirt was way too big, I welcomed the blanket feel I'd needed to keep me covered and shapeless. "Thanks. That helps. Feels like armor and a hug all in one."

Bastien's eyes were mournful as he cupped my face. "What else can I do? How can I make it less awful?"

I buried my face in his chest. "Just be here while it sucks, and don't make me talk about it."

"I can do that." His arms were strong, and banded around me with a protective strength that calmed my worries. When my lips found his, he made these sweet indulgent noises that showed me how much he'd wanted me to be near him. It was a heady thing to be needed like that, and by someone who didn't seem to need anything.

"Third wheel in the room, guys. Keep the slurping noises to a minimum while you suck each other's faces." Judah sat up, rubbing his eyes.

I broke from Bastien and ran to my BFF. "Judah! Are you alright?"

"I'm not tied to the ground anymore, so I'm amazing." He hugged me tight, and neither of us wanted to let go. "What about you?"

"I don't care about me! What the crap happened that you landed yourself in Avalon?"

Judah's hand gripped the back of my head, and then slipped to my shoulders, no doubt trying to familiarize himself with my new body that had possessed a hump for most of our friendship. "A few disfigured soldier dudes broke into the apartment and snatched me out of my bed. I'm still breathing a sigh of relief that Jill wasn't home from her shift yet."

I moved to the window and opened it to let in a bird that landed on the sill. He flew in and perched on my shoulder, chirping tidings of joy and blessings on my feathers. I grabbed Judah's stolen glasses off my table and handed them to him, both of us sighing with relief, now that the perfect picture of Judah was complete. My posture lifted as I sat on my knees on the mattress. "Jill moved in? You two are still together?"

Judah nodded, holding his hand out to touch my bird. "I couldn't afford the rent on my own after you moved out."

"I hope you put a more romantic spin on it than that," I joked. "She's a sweet girl."

"Left me for a few weeks when I disappeared, way back when the whole Avalon thing blew up. But we got back together. I'm in permanent doghouse mode since I didn't come back with an engagement ring, so I cook dinner every night and do most of the cleaning, but she pays half the rent, so it works."

"Tell me more of this sweeping romance you two have," I said with a hint of dreaminess to curb my sarcasm. My fingers were clasped under my chin, and a cheesy smile was plastered across my features.

"Well, I'm sure she thinks I'm dead by now. They took me at least three weeks ago. It's hard to keep track. Trashed the place in the struggle to get me out."

"I hope you made it hurt."

"I so did. They were all, 'I'm gonna kidnap you to lure Rosie into a trap,' and I was like, 'I'll straight up Schwarzenegger your asses! I'll fill your inbox with penis enlargement spam! I'll reprogram your computer so it crashes every time you save a document!'" Judah demonstrated with a few punches in the air. "They eventually won, but they know I'm a beast."

I laughed and threw my arms around him again. "You're a terrifying programmer, that's for sure." I let out a stream of laughter mixed with elation at the familiar back and forth. "So much of my life is different now; I barely remember who I am most days. This? You being here? I feel it now. I can feel myself still in there, thanks to you."

Judah's cheek lifted into a smile that was pressed next to mine. My bird hopped from his shoulder to mine, and back again, chirping excitedly. "Aw, you're still you. I could recognize you a mile away, even with your new funky eye and this whole Beauty Queen Barbie look you've got going now."

I laughed at the truth of that statement. "You loved me even when I was walleyed and had a hump."

"Of course I did. You were the best rapper I'd ever met. You've seen pictures of Biggie. He's no princess, and he was still awesome." Judah pulled back with a frown. "Don't tell me you traded your rap skillz for this new prom queen body. Please tell me Shorty's still gonna be a thug."

I grinned at Judah as a dozen more birds flew in through the window. Finally I felt waves of my personality that had nothing to do with survival or power struggles or hot guys flow through me. The simplicity of friendship revived the parts of me that needed rejuvenation.

Judah took the beat, climbing off the bed so he could throw up fake gang signs while he rapped in style. We had this song so down.

Bastien stood awkwardly at the side of the bed, not knowing how to invade our dynamic that hadn't skipped a beat. His eyes were wide at our goofiness, his eyebrows raised at our synchronized antics. We rapped to our hearts' content, letting 2Pac lead us home. I threw my hands up, ignoring Link and Mad, who strolled into my room without knocking.

We cut the outro short because Link started hooting and hollering that we were awesome. To be fair, we totally were. I threw my arms around Judah, who squeezed me tight at the sight of the newcomers. "See? You're still you, no matter where they put you or what you look like. Life's good, because we've always got each other – two thugs throwing shade in Avalon."

I let out a nervous laugh of elation as the birds chirped around me, hopping and flapping their wings. "I think I needed to hear that. Thanks, Judah."

The Untouchables each eyed me with bewildered looks of amusement and wariness. "So tha's your mate, Judah, yeah?" Judah had seen Link murder the soldiers who'd held him hostage one by one, but they hadn't had much in the way of conversation, since Kerdik had knocked the three out for much of the journey home.

Judah gave me a look to ask if these guys were cool, and I nodded. He stuck his hand out and shook Link's with a firm, welcoming grip. "Hey, man. Thanks for the rescue. I thought we were goners for sure."

"Aye. It's no trouble. Are ye well?" Link nodded, releasing Judah's hand. He kept his eyes affixed to my bestie to size up just what kind of weirdo Judah was.

The awesome brand of weirdo, that's what kind.

Judah grinned and turned his head to me. "Dude's legit Irish, like from the motherland. Totally cool."

"He's from Éireland – that's the other country here. Do *not* ask him where he keeps his Lucky Charms. You'll get penis jokes for days. Learned that one the hard way."

Link clapped his hands and threw his head back in a laugh. "'The hard way?' Tha's brilliant."

Judah jabbed my side with his elbow. "Are Éirish penis jokes better than ours? I might do it just to get some new material."

I pointed to Mad, who made no move to greet Judah, or speak. "This is Lucky Charms, Part Two – Madigan. Mad, this is my bestie from Common, Judah."

Mad was no-nonsense, as usual. "So he's staying around? Or are we taking him up to Common?"

I shrugged, but Judah was firm. "I'll go back up when Rosie does. It was a bad idea to split up the first time, Ro. We're not going through that again."

Mad nodded once. "Fine, but he's sleeping in a different room if he's staying here. No fiancée of mine is sleeping with another man, unless it's Bastien."

I groaned as Judah hooted his shock. "You're engaged? You're engaged to Murdering Éirishman Number 2? No offense, Ro, but he's... What's the word? Terrifying."

Link guffawed, indignant. "No, he's not! Mad's only formidable. Wouldn't ye rather be Link the Terrifying? Way better sound to it than Madigan the Formidable." He stuck out his tongue in a grimace, as if Mad's moniker tasted sour on his lips.

I rolled my eyes. "It's not a real engagement. It was just for show, to keep my uncle from trying to marry me and get me pregnant."

Judah stumbled back and sat on the bed. "Hold up. You're fake engaged, you found more family, but they're apparently disgusting, you got a neck tattoo, and your birth mom's a kidnapping villain?"

"That about sums it up, yeah. But we're not fake engaged anymore, Mad," I reminded him. "You broke that off when you left the first time."

Judah jerked his thumb toward Bastien, who'd moved to affix his arm around my hips. That was about as subtle as Bastien got when he was staking his territory. "Then why's Bastien acting like he's the husband? I don't get it. Start from the beginning."

"I *am* the husband," Bastien declared, making my spine straighten. "Or I will be, anyways." At his pronouncement, the birds went wild, some of them flying out to be the first to spread the news to the wild kingdom that the *Voix* was getting married.

I massaged my forehead. "Oh, jeez. Now they're telling all the animals that."

"Good. I hope they do. I hope they spontaneously grow the ability to speak to more people than just you, so everyone knows that you're with me."

"If you keep this up, I'm going to start believing you're in love with me, and then where would we be?"

"Married, that's where. Exactly where I want us."

"Papa!" Annabelle cried, crashing into Mad from behind. She clung to his leg until he picked her up with a frustrated sigh, glaring at me. She flung her arms around his neck and squeezed. "Papa, ye left before I was finished eating!"

"Aye. I told ye I would if ye didn't hurry it up. Ye eat too slow."

Annabelle turned her head to me and smiled, pressing her cheek to Mad's. "Auntie Rose, ye came back?"

"I did. And this is your new friend Judah. He's a brave knight from Common."

Annabelle's eyes widened. "A knight from Common? Papa, is he a good knight, or an evil one?"

Mad sized up Judah with a hard stare. "He's harmless. You're safe with him, so long as no one attacks." More of my birds flew in through the window, landing on my shoulders, and hopping onto the arms of whoever I was talking to. They were so excited I was back, and wanted to be part of the action.

Still, Annabelle didn't let go. She clung to Mad with her arms and legs, no doubt scared that he'd been gone for so long. His thick forearm supported her featherweight easily as he leveled his hard stare at me. "Are ye alright, Rosie?"

I nodded once. "You can thank Kerdik and Link for that. They saved the day, for sure."

Link took no joy in being the victor. "I still don't understand why she lured Draper, Mad and Bastien to the castle, when Lane was in the opposite direction. She had to know it would be them who'd come to the castle, and she couldn't touch them. It makes no sense."

"She was probably hoping I'd come with the ring or the Jewels of Good Fortune."

"She knows Urien would never allow tha."

Judah spoke up from his seat on the bed. "She took us to the middle of nowhere to see if Rosie could find us." He held up his fist to me for a quick pound. "Rosie could find a bent needle in a stack of good needles without a blink. I knew you'd find us."

My fist fell to my side, and I paled. "The soldiers said that was the plan? To see if I could find you?"

Judah nodded, confused as to why I looked sick to my stomach all of a sudden. "Yeah. But you found us, Ro. We're safe now. Not Remy or Damond, but I know you came as quick as you could." He looked down. "They were good guys, too. It was hard because he couldn't talk, but to his last breath Remy seemed like a decent guy. We would write notes in the dirt to each other." Judah looked as if he was seeing the scene in his mind. "He said he was your healer, and that if I got free, to tell you that he was grateful you let him in your service. Said he was your knight."

I closed my eyes at the painful slash that marked my

heart. Of course Remy was grateful, even until death. That's just who he was. "He should've been cursing my name. If he hadn't been affiliated with me, he wouldn't have been taken. He was helping Lane, making sure Reyn was healthy for the trek across Avalon."

Bastien's grip on me tightened, bringing me in for a hug I needed. "He died knowing he'd chosen the right side. If he could do it all over again, he wouldn't hesitate to go where you went."

"And I get to live with that guilt. He would still be alive if he hadn't followed me to Province 9."

"I don't think he'd been alive for a long time before he met you." Bastien was kind to me, gentle when I seemed perpetually fragile. I didn't used to be so emotional, but having the people you care about drop like flies whenever you turn your back can wear down even the most stoic girl. "Remy loved you, babe."

I nodded into Bastien's shirt. "And now he's dead because of it. I'd get your wills together now, guys." I turned to the others, determined not to tear up; I didn't want to scare Annabelle by letting blood stream down my face. "Could we send a medal or something to Remy's parents in his honor, like how we did when Montel died?"

"Of course. I'll make sure that happens," Bastien said softly.

I shook my head at the state of the world, wishing so many things could be different. "Judah, you're saying

Morgan wanted to see if I could find you guys? That was the whole point of the trap?"

Judah nodded. "No fair. You joined a gang without me?" He motioned to my neck tattoo.

"Sort of," I admitted. I rubbed my temples. "You guys, this is bad. Now Morgan knows I have the Compass ability, which was something I didn't want her to figure out. She's going to use me to find something. I don't know what, but something. She knows I have more than half the jewels. She knows where the others are. What could she want to find that she doesn't already know who has it?"

Bastien tensed at the new development. "I don't know. She only wants power, and she has about half of it, judging by the census we're taking." His hand clutched mine. "Not out of my sight. I'm firm on that."

"Oh, fine. It's almost like you're telling me to have ice cream for dinner. Being around you? Not the chore you're making it seem."

"I'll remember you said that when you're begging to go do something dangerous, and I won't let you."

"Aw, I love when you think you can control me. It's so cute."

Judah sized us up. "Wow. He's not a bad match for you, Ro." He looked over at Bastien. "Not for nothing, but I thought you were a tool when you first kidnapped us. Now that you've got Rosie practically swooning with Stockholm Syndrome, I'll give you a second chance."

Link moved in and scooped me in a gentle hug. "I just

came up to check on ye, then I have to go back out. Are ye alright, wee Rose?"

"I am. You saved the day." I grinned up at him, trying to let everyone know that I didn't want to talk about the awfulness of it all. "Now, no more killing, okay? That was about all the murdering I can handle."

"I'd do it all over again to keep ye safe. You're one of us now. No one puts their hands on an Untouchable's lady." Link smooched my lips, earning a contented look from Bastien that his brothers doted on me.

I ruffled Link's hair. "Love you," I said, earning a raised eyebrow from Judah, who was no doubt wondering, as I was, just what the crap had happened to my life.

Link pulled back with a grin that was almost bashful. "Aye. If you're alright, I'll go back to the men and see what soldiers we can drum up. If Morgan's planning something, I want us ready next time."

Mad shifted Annabelle on his hip, his hard gaze meeting mine after he snarled at the three birds on his shoulder. "I failed ye again. I'll not fall for Morgan's traps next time."

I knew Mad didn't like to be touched, so I resisted hugging him or kissing his cheek. "You didn't fail. You did everything you could. I'm glad you made it back to me safely."

Mad put Annabelle down. "Go into the hallway. I have to talk to Auntie Rose for a mo."

"You'll come back out soon?" Annabelle questioned, scared to be without him.

"Aye. Remember what I taught ye." He pulled a dagger from her apron and wound her tiny fingers around the handle. "If anyone tries to snatch at ye, through the stomach and drag the blade sideways."

"Jeez, Mad! You can't give a child a knife like that!"

Mad quirked his eyebrow at me. "I had more than this little pig-sticker at her age."

I rolled my eyes, exasperated. "Yes, let's try to get her childhood closer to yours. That's a great idea."

Mad patted Annabelle on the head, and closed her out in the hallway. He fixed his eyes on me, his shoulders tensed. "Ye were supposed to be my wife, and they all knew it. Ye wear our mark, but it didn't do nothing to save ye. I told ye I'd keep ye safe, and I failed again."

I couldn't take his matter-of-fact self-loathing. I didn't want this to be the truth he told himself. "Mad, stop it. Seriously, it's not your fault. Morgan is who she is. I didn't keep you safe, either. Link got this slice on his arm in the fight, no doubt." I motioned to a small cut on Link's forearm, which he scoffed at.

"Tha's from a tree. No one dared touch me."

Mad held my gaze. "Point is, listen to Bastien. Don't go anywhere without one of us on ye."

I nodded, if only to make him feel better. "Okay, Mad. If that's what you want."

Judah stood, reminding the men that there was a new

addition to the castle. "I'm going to hang with Lane for a while. See what she needs." He pointed to Link, who raised his chin. "And for the record, you go ahead and slit the throats of anyone who hurts my mom like that, or my best friend. I know you don't know me, but I straight up love you, man. Thanks for coming in and getting us out of there before they took Rosie like how they took Lane."

I loved when Judah claimed Lane as his mother. It made it feel like we were brother and sister, which part of me always wished we were.

Link nodded to Judah, giving him a small smile at his declaration. "Aye. I'll end any man who touches our wee Rose. Mind ye remember tha."

Judah held up his hands to prove their innocence. "Never been a thing between us like that, so you don't need to worry. I've got a girlfriend back home."

"I'm coming with," I said to Judah, wanting to escape the serious conversations. When Bastien opened the door for me, I kissed his cheek. "You can come, but you don't have to. I know you've got stuff you want to take care of with Link, training the men and whatnot."

Bastien yanked on my ponytail, jerking my head up so I couldn't escape his frustration. "It's like you didn't hear a word we said. Not out of my sight."

"Oh, right. Okay, then. You'll be bored, though." I knelt down and gave Annabelle a hug, carefully tucking the dagger back into its sheath before placing it in her apron's pocket. "Make sure the soldiers mind their manners, and that they listen to your papa, okay?"

Her head bobbed, her pin-straight black ponytail swishing up and down. "Okay, Auntie Rose. Uncle Bastien, can I have a cookie?" She giggled at the birds that flapped their wings on her dainty arms.

Bastien knelt down on her other side and kissed her cheek. "I think that would be okay. But only after supper tonight, alright?"

Mad growled. "No sugar. I already said tha downstairs. You're asking these pushovers because you're hoping they'll cave. Sugar makes your brain soft when it should be sharp."

Annabelle sighed with discontent. "Aye, Papa."

Bastien gave her tiny arm a light pinch. "Listen to your Papa, then. Gotta make sure you eat enough healthy food. Big meals mean big muscles." He slapped his meaty bicep and growled at her with a grin. "You're supposed to have my back, right?"

Annabelle nodded, loving being part of the team. "Okay. I'll watch Papa while you're gone."

"Good girl. Make sure he smiles at least twice today, got it?"

She saluted Bastien, taking her post seriously.

After everything we'd been through, it was nice to know there were still little girls in the world who dreamed about cookies.

26

LANE'S TWO SONS

"I really don't need any more water, Reyn. I'm feeling much better." Lane was still moving slowly, but she managed to stand from her bed with only a muted noise of discomfort.

"I'll get you the healer again. You're clearly in pain." Reyn wrapped a blanket around her shoulders and kissed her temple. It was sweet to watch him hover; it was far better than when he hadn't been able to process anything. "Bastien, will you watch them?"

"Of course, brother."

As soon as Reyn left the room, Lane rolled back her shoulders and discarded the blanket on the bed with the ten others. "He's obsessed with bringing me blankets. It's sweet, but I can't be the sick person anymore. Someone give me a job I can do from in here. I can't go back out until my face is healed, but I'm not useless! I've got a funeral to whip up and a nation to calm down."

Draper put the blanket around her shoulders again, wrapping her in it like a towel at the beach as he rubbed her arms. He was tall and princely looking, appearing more Lane's age than the son she'd adopted him to be. "I've already started making arrangements for Damond. I've had his things sent to Duke Henri in Province 2, and the Wildmen are coming up with a dirge to invoke reverence and peace into the hearts of the people at the funeral. All of that is my job. Damond is my brother."

I didn't love that Remy wouldn't get a grand funeral, but in the end, he was my knight, not an actual royal. Still, I held the unrest in my heart at his death, wondering how long it would take for a wound of this caliber to heal.

Lane was irate. "But I'm the one who let Damond come here! I should be the one handling his affairs. And I sent all the people from Province 8 here. Do we have the land for everyone?"

"We can make room." Draper was kind, but firm. "Whatever you want to do can be done from the bed. You know Jean-Luc told you to lie down."

"I'm fine," she said, chin raised. I knew that stubbornness anywhere.

I giggled. "Whoa. Is that what I look like when I'm being bull-headed?"

"To a T," Bastien replied. "Like mother, like daughter."

I loved Bastien for declaring Lane as my mother, and not Morgan.

Judah knew Lane's temper was about to flare, so he picked up a piece of parchment from the messy desk, welcoming the five birds that perched on his shoulders. "What are these?"

"That's a speech for Urien to give later today in Town Square, announcing Prince Damond's death. Plus he's got to deal with the growing tension. There's been frustration with too many people trying to share the two water sources we have."

"What about Master Kerdik? He said he wanted to help. Can't he just make us a new well?" Draper suggested. He'd been withdrawn, not wanting to talk about Damond's death, though it was clear by the perpetual wrinkle between his eyebrows that he thought of his brother often.

Lane and I both shook our heads as if they were tied to the same string. "No," I ruled. "Kerdik's awesome, but we can't be a nation who relies on him."

Lane chimed in with, "Master Kerdik's benevolence turns on a dime. When Rosie moves back to Common, who's to say he won't join her, and leave us to our drying wells? We have to be able to sustain ourselves on our own. Otherwise, we risk total devastation if he leaves."

Bastien scoffed, offering his arm for Lane to lean on as he led her to her desk and helped her to sit down. He took great care transporting her, not hesitating to dole out the gentleness our family needed. "Kerdik's not moving to Common with us."

I held up my hands to show my innocence. "I didn't say it. Lane did."

Bastien stared down at Lane. "Kerdik's staying in Faîte. I've had about all I can take from him. Rosie's my girl-friend, and when we move somewhere safer than Avalon, she'll be my wife. A marriage takes two people, not three."

Lane's head snapped to me. "Your wife, eh? Is that so? Looks like you're going to have to do some serious grov-eling if you want my blessing or Urien's for her hand."

Bastien narrowed one eye at her, ignoring the four dozen birds who chirped wildly their happiness that we were getting married. "I'll grovel when it's time. Until then, I'll watch your daughter to make sure she's safe, and I'll guard your castle to make sure no one snatches at you again. Now sit down and take it easy."

Judah distracted Lane by asking her question after question about the wells, until I remembered what I'd been trying to draw up in the saferoom when I'd been waiting out the Sluagh. "I was thinking about aqueducts," I interjected.

"That's what I was going to suggest," Judah nodded. "But what's the building equipment like around here? Better than Ancient Rome?"

"On par, at least." Lane's eyes grew to the size of saucers. "I didn't even think of that. But I don't remember the specifics of your high school World History project. We have limited resources and manpower, so we can't afford to get anything wrong. Can you draft something up for Urien? Like, something you're sure will work?"

Judah and I mimed putting our thinking caps on in unison. "On it," Judah confirmed with confidence. "We used hollowed-out Lincoln Logs for the actual ducts, because it was to scale of the houses we built out of milk cartons."

"But we don't want wood. We can use stone. That, we can ask Kerdik for help with. And if he's not up for it, the masons can figure it out."

"Can someone help us out by drawing a map of the province?" Judah tore off a long chunk of parchment and spread it out on the floor.

"Lane and I can do that," Draper offered, taking the ink pot and quill from the desk so he could kneel next to Judah. He shook Judah's hand with a composed expression. "I'm Draper, by the way. Lane's son."

Judah slapped Draper on the back. "Laney, you've got some 'splaining to do. Who you been making babies with, girl? I thought I was your only son."

Lane smiled, and I could tell she wasn't expecting to be able to find anything to grin about this soon. That was the magic of Judah. "Before I left Avalon to live in Common when Rosie was a baby, I was raising my nephew. Now that I'm back, I finally was able to adopt him, just like I always wanted. Now he and Rosie are brother and sister, just like the two of you were raised to be." She winced when

Bastien helped her off the chair so he could lower her to the floor next to the parchment. "Draper, Judah grew up down the street from us with his mother. Now he and Rosie have an apartment together at the college they go to."

I didn't want to rain on the parade by telling her that Jill probably couldn't afford the place on her own, so Judah and I were technically without our tiny haven.

Judah quirked his eyebrow at Draper. "I always wanted a big brother to sneak me smokes and teach me how to pick up chicks. I already know how to change a tire and unclog a drain, but having a big brother to show me how to hang drywall would be cool. Do you know how to do that?"

Draper was surprised how easily Judah took to the idea of being invited into the family we'd crafted. I winced that Draper still thought of himself as the black sheep, perplexed when anyone smiled at him without agenda. "I'm sure I could teach you that. You're right, pumpkin. He's great. I think we'll keep him around."

I squinted at Draper as Lane started drawing out where the forest was, and moved her quill inward on the parchment from there. "You're not teaching Judah how to pick up women." I sighed in Judah's direction. "Draper used to run a brothel. He's reformed now, courtesy of Lane tearing him a new one."

"Dude, why does everyone's job sound cooler than mine?"

"Hey, now. Being a Geek Squad techy is cool."

Judah rolled his eyes as he sat on the floor next to Lane. "Yes. I have to fend off the ladies with a stick. I whip out my name badge, and they fall all over themselves trying to get at me."

Lane wrapped Judah in a motherly hug and ruffled his hair as the birds hopped around us. "Who said my baby boy's not cool? I think you're the best Common has to offer. No contest, Judah's the man."

I fanned myself and donned my girliest voice. "Judah's going to be at the party? I have to get in now! If Judah's there, then it's gonna be off the hook. I hope he notices me."

Judah's neck shrunk as he indulged Lane in the hug he would never push away. His own mother was nice enough, but she wasn't the same lovey goofball as Lane. "Okay, okay. There's enough of me to go around, ladies."

"I think the northern quarter's bigger than that, Lane," Draper said, moving his finger along the map that was slowly coming together.

"You know, you're right. It's this rectangle shape of the paper. It's messing with my brain mojo."

"On it." Judah hacked off the end, making it square for her. "Can't have the brain mojo being scrambled."

"My hero," she crooned.

He batted his hand at her. "You're just saying that because I'm amazing." Judah sat back on his heels while Draper and Lane worked on the map.

Lane was happy to be useful, comforted by the knowledge that the soldiers hadn't been able to take her work ethic from her. Despite the demons that might haunt her for years to come, she was happiest when she had a trail to blaze, a project to tackle, and a nation to save. My Lane was fantastic at rescuing whole worlds – she'd saved mine on more than one occasion.

Judah crossed his arms over his chest as he stared at me across Lane's bent-over form. "So, you met your mom, who's evil somehow. You have a dad somewhere in this place. Is he cool?"

"Only the coolest. Richard the Lionhearted, in the flesh."

"You've got a new brother, who's not quite Geek Squad cool, but he's got his own thing going. You could totally win an episode of *Cribs*, with this palace you've got going for you. Though, it's no one-bedroom apartment, that's for sure. You've got a fake ex-fiancé and a boyfriend, which is quite the achievement, you dog. Plus you joined a gang. Is that about it?"

"That's the whole story, just about."

Bastien scoffed. "That's nothing like the whole story." He took it upon himself to tell Judah my life in Avalon from the beginning, catching him up on the highlights of my journey that he'd missed. Judah was quiet, commenting only when a new term hit him that didn't make sense. Judah had always been an excellent student, and I could see him mentally preparing for some sort of exam.

When Kerdik entered, most of the room stiffened at his presence, but Judah crossed the room and wrapped him in a tight hug. I covered my mouth to stifle a laugh at Kerdik's stiff body and eyes that were wide with alarm. Judah's gratitude was heartfelt as he squeezed Kerdik. "Thanks for rescuing us, dude."

27

AQUEDUCTS AND MEETING SUPERMAN

Kerdik raised his eyebrow at Judah's lack of fear. "I'm Master Kerdik. And you're Rosie's Commoner friend who shares a bed with her."

Judah laughed and clapped his hands twice as he stepped back. "Oh, please make that my title. That's too funny. Or you can call me Judah, Grand Master Kerdik." He offered his hand to Kerdik, but Kerdik looked at his palm as if it was an annoying fly.

"Be nice, now. You're going to get along with Judah," I informed him. "There's not a second option tucked in there."

Kerdik rolled his eyes and shook Judah's hand. "How nice to have you here, taking up space in Rosie's bed."

Judah did a stage whisper out the side of his mouth. "Dude's skin is green! That is so cool!"

"I know, right? That's what I said when I first met him."

Kerdik looked on Judah with new appreciation. "What are you working on?"

"Aqueducts. It's one of the advancements that moved Ancient Rome ahead of its time."

"I don't know of these aqueducts. What are they?"

Judah motioned to the map, which was about halfway filled in. "They take the problem of centralized water and distribute it to where everyone can get some. Then there won't be any more long treks to the wells, and we could even talk about getting running water indoors down the road. That's if the initial setup goes smoothly, of course."

"Running water indoors? Like, in the palace?" Kerdik scoffed. "That's not a thing."

Judah and I both nodded, then I voiced my concern. "The problem I ran into when I was puzzling this out was that the water sources aren't raised. So during the times of year when the water level is low, the aqueducts might not be super helpful."

"You need the well raised? Like, on a hill or something?" Kerdik inquired. "I can do that for you."

Judah shook his head. "No, like actually raised, not a pail of water raised in a bucket or something. I didn't realize the wells were at ground level, though maybe that's the first thing I should've asked. It's alright. We can figure it out."

I pointed to Kerdik's affronted expression. "Kerdik's an elemental, so he can legit raise a well up a few feet by making it be on a hill."

"No way. You're friends with an elemental? What level?" Judah's mind was in full-on D&D mode, which was when he was at his most precious.

"Level Infinity. Kerdik's the king of like, all the things. Except Province 9. My dad's the king of that." I smirked up at the doorway when my father entered. "Dad, meet Judah, King of the Geek Squad."

Judah scrambled to stand and brushed his hand down his shirt in an attempt to look presentable before he extended his hand. "Pleasure to meet you, sir."

My dad postured, looking every bit as kingly as his title proclaimed. "The pleasure's mine. I hear you're responsible for looking after my Rosie up in Common. Thank you for keeping her safe with Lane for me."

Judah seemed to swell with pride. Like me, he had a bit of a dad complex, and beamed at making a good impression as Superman shook his hand. "That was all Lane, to be honest. Rosie had my back every bit as much as I had hers."

"Modest," Dad commented. "I like this one."

Judah spoke out of the corner of his mouth to me in a loud whisper. "Dude, an actual king likes me and thanked me for keeping a princess safe. I win all the points ever."

Lane and I shared a giggle. "You know everyone can hear you when you do that, right?"

"No, they can't. It's my superpower." Judah sat back down between Lane and me, studying the map that was nearing fruition.

"I can't believe how many other provinces joined us. We're barely Province 9 anymore," Lane remarked as she scribbled on the map.

I spoke slowly, meeting her eyes as the new idea hit us at the same time. "If we're not Province 9, then maybe we should have a new name, so everyone's included. The land should belong to all of us."

"Province 10," Lane decreed.

Dad nodded, his jaw going tight as he factored in the new information. "I think that's a splendid idea. It will keep any sort of elitist attitude from forming and dividing the people further. Everyone in Avalon will be in either Province 1 with Morgan, or Province 10 with us."

"Us," I echoed, touched that I was part of such a legacy. We were renaming a whole people, and I got to be part of that process.

Judah let out a low whistle. "Wow. I barely understand what's going on, but that felt important." His eyes drifted back to the map as it started to come to fruition under Draper and Lane's careful measurements. The others chatted quietly around us, but I heard Judah's low humming. The tune both of us knew by heart relaxed my shoulders and made me feel so much more at home than I had in a while. Funny how music could do that to you.

I started quietly singing along to his humming, knowing by heart every single lyric Lost and Forgotten had ever recorded. "'You say I've found a new road to drive down. We both know we can't go there together. You found a new car, but I've moved on, driving my old Cadillac to something better.'"

Judah joined me at the chorus, and we harmonized almost as seamlessly as the perfect musicians on the album had. "'You taste like spring, but I prefer whiskey. How glad I'll be when you don't want to kiss me. It was good while it lasted, but now that it's done...'" We paused for the solo on the bass guitar that totally made the song, playing air guitar together to the same beat. "'You say I'm the loser, but losing you's where I won.'"

Judah and I grinned at each other, grateful that after everything we'd been through, we still knew the lyrics to our favorite songs. We hadn't forgotten the important things in life.

Lane dabbed at her eyes with her sleeve, waving me off when I asked her what was wrong. "Nothing, baby. I'm just being emotional. I worry all the time. Are you eating your vegetables? Are you making the right kind of friends? Are you safe? I forget to worry about if you're still able to play. Hearing you sing after all we've been through?" She melted as Draper pulled her into his arms so she had a safe place to unburden herself. "I think I needed that."

Judah started yodeling to break the tension, making Lane and me burst out into fits of giggles.

Bastien was on edge, gathering me closer every time Judah high-fived me, which was whenever we agreed on the measurements or anything concerning the aqueducts. I wanted to explain for the millionth time that Judah was no one to be worried about, but it was no use. I'd kissed Kerdik when we weren't totally together yet, so I understood Bastien's insecurity, and decided to be patient with it. I kissed my boyfriend's cheek, just to make it clear that we were very much together, and that no matter how many penises were around me, he was the only guy I wanted in my bed anymore.

When Reyn came back, I thought he might have a heart attack. "Are you serious? Get her off the floor!" I was about to blow him off with a "Lane's fine, you drama king," but his scared expression closed my mouth. He drew Lane up as if we'd thrown her down on the ground and told her she was a bad girl. His arms cocooned her, as if she was too fragile for such things as company. Maybe she was; it was hard to tell with Lane.

Her voice was quiet, calming him instead of letting him soothe her. "I'm alright, Reyn. We were just talking about improvements to make on the province."

"You can do that when you're better, which Jean-Luc didn't say you are. Staying in bed is what he recommended for you."

"She's fine to have a conversation. But maybe not on the floor is a good rule for any duchess. I need to examine her again." Jean-Luc met my eyes. *"How are you, your grace?"*

"I'm better than fine. They didn't hurt me like they did Lane."

Lane's finger pointed to the door. "Out you go, both of you. Rosie, Judah, out. You, too, Draper."

My mouth fell open. "What? Why would I have to go? I'm being helpful."

"Of course you are, but Jean-Luc wants to examine me again, and I don't want you hearing the details through his mind. You don't need to live through what I had to."

I lowered my chin, but didn't argue. Lane's body was her own, and she should have the say-so in who knew the details about the roughing up she'd gone through. "Whatever makes you more comfortable. You know I love you, right?"

Lane had the presence of mind to shoot me a gentle smile. "I know, baby. But I want you to stay my baby as long as you can. Hearing about all this? It'll age you too quickly. I don't want to be part of anything that makes you stop singing."

Carefully, and with Reyn watching like a hawk, I wrapped my arms around her. "You're my Supermom. It's okay to be a human once in a while, too. You'll holler if you need anything? I mean anything at all? Four in the morning and you need to know who the lead singer of the Lost and Forgotten is, you'll come get me?"

"You'll be the first stop." When I yawned over her shoulder, she motioned to Bastien. "The birds overdid it. She might need to lie down."

I frowned at her as I pulled back. "Okay, I'm not an actual baby, just because I'm your baby. I'm fine. Ready for anything."

"Good," Kerdik interjected. "Because I could use more

information on this water system you and your little friend have going."

I thrilled at the feeling of being needed for something academic. It was a rush I didn't often get, and I relished every second of it. "Of course. Happy to help."

Kerdik held out his elbow to escort me, but Bastien moved me so I was on his right, and Kerdik at his left. It was territorial, sure, but I understood. Bastien was done fooling around, and done being apart. We'd lost each other too many times for a cool and casual slide into something more serious. When my arm looped through Bastien's, he tightened his bicep, pinning my hand to his side to ensure that no one – not even Kerdik – could snatch at me ever again.

28

THIS IS JUDAH

"I still don't know," Kerdik sighed, looking at the detailed drawing on the parchment we'd spread out on the overlarge dark wood dining room table. It could easily seat sixteen people, but today it was just the four of us standing around it, frowning at the map. After Lane kicked us out, we'd set up in here, working on the new water system. "Where will the water end up?"

Judah pointed to a spot near the palace on the map. "Here would be great, but it has to be on a spot lower than the well. Otherwise the flow will be all wrong."

Kerdik frowned. "I don't want the palace to have the lowest ground. It doesn't send the right message. The palace should be on high ground – a city on a hill."

Kerdik and Judah went back and forth on different locations for the end point of the water tunnels, speaking like coworkers who were comfortable enough for a studious back and forth. It was cute, actually. I loved that Judah was fitting in pretty seamlessly with the people in my Avalon life.

Bastien studied the map and pointed to a cluster of trees. "This is where the wall is going to go, once it's all finished. You guys didn't take into account that our province is going to have a wall."

I slapped my forehead, and took the quill Judah surrendered to me. "You're totally right. We're about here on the construction right now," I said, drawing a line to indicate the parts of the wall that were already up. Then I drew a dotted line where the rest of the wall would be, once finished. I made to hand the quill back to Judah. "The wall's twelve feet high by about fifteen inches thick."

I expected Judah to take the quill and jot down the measurements in his neat handwriting, but instead he wrapped his fist around mine and slowly wrote out the specifications with me. That was the good thing about Judah. He didn't draw attention to my shortcomings, but he didn't let me off easy, either. We were a team, and he didn't mind taking the handicap that was all me.

Kerdik and Bastien were quiet at the help Judah gave without a conversation, taking mental notes that this was how I needed help to be offered, so I didn't walk away feeling like a dummy.

Judah dipped the quill back into the ink pot, and hovered our joined fists over the map with a frown. "There needs to be some kind of flourish at the end, some kind of

'Bite me, suckers. I just built you the first water system in Avalon!' There's a huge one, the Trevi Fountain, at the end of the aqueduct lines in Rome. It's got sculptures made of marble, and it's like a beacon for the city. It should encourage the people, so that when they look at it, they feel unstoppable. Like, 'Dude, this was a hard day, but look at where we live. No other place in Avalon has anything as super way awesome as that.'"

Kerdik tried to hide his amusement at Judah's candid speech, but eventually lost to his smirk. "You sound like Rosie. You even swivel your head like her."

"No, no, no. Rosie talks like me. She learned all her moves from me, because I'm awesome."

I guffawed. "Says the dude who can't get through an Eminem or Macklemore song without stopping to take a breath."

"Those dudes are superhuman! I don't know how they rap without breathing like that!"

I blew on my nails and polished them on my shirt. "Child's play." I pointed with my free hand to the courtyard in front of the palace on the map. "How about here?"

"Works for me." He moved our hands down to the parchment so we drew a circle, writing "Fountain" in the center. Judah and I put the quill in the ink and dropped our hands so he could scratch his head. "Do we have any sculptors who could take on the task of making a totally wicked fountain?"

Kerdik shot Judah a withering look. "Talk about child's

play. Something grand like you're suggesting would only take me a few hours, as opposed to several craftsmen, who would have to spend months with a chisel, only to get the details subpar in the end. I can do that."

I shook my head. "You're doing too much as it is. These aqueducts? They have to be formed and then placed properly. I don't want you exhausting yourself. I mean it. We shouldn't be asking you for this much magic."

"But I can get the measurements more perfect than anyone else can, and I can do it faster." His eyebrows furrowed. "Why won't you let me help your country?"

I debated pulling Kerdik into the hallway for a private conversation, but knew Bastien would have a cow if I stepped a foot outside of the dining hall we were standing in. "Because you'll resent us. You'll despise Lane for asking you for this much help. When they sing Lane's praises or my dad's, you'll get pissed that it's not your name they chant, and you'll take it out on them. Or worse, you'll destroy the water system completely, and then we're right back where we started."

Kerdik's stare would have made me wither, were I not spot on. "I'm not like that anymore."

"Since when?" Bastien countered, his hand moving to the small of my back, as it did now whenever Kerdik addressed me.

"You want me to be less selfish, so I volunteer to help with something you actually need, and this is the thanks I get?"

"Thank you," I said with a polite bob of my head. "But think this through. I don't want our province dependent on you."

"You won't be! I'll set up the system, and leave it alone. After the aqueducts are set up, the people can repair them if they break down over time. You're not dependent on me; I'm just giving the new Province 10 a head start."

I pursed my lips as I thought through his logic. "Okay. I guess that makes sense. So you're throwing your chips in with Lane, then? You're officially behind Province 10?"

Kerdik tossed his hands up in exasperation. "Don't you see me at all? I'd follow you anywhere, making sure you had water, food and shelter. You're their princess, but you've been my queen since I first saw you in that storm. I came to Province 10 for you, but I'm staying because it's bigger than that now. Morgan needs to be stopped. When I saw what the soldiers did to you and Lane, I got it. I finally understood. If I don't help you stop Morgan, then every man's treasure is sure to be snatched at. I wouldn't wish the horror I felt seeing you manhandled like that on anyone."

Judah let out a low whistle and stepped back, lifting his hands up to indicate that he was staying out of whatever mess I'd put my foot in this time.

Bastien's arm coiled around my hips, and he leveled his finger at Kerdik. "You'll stop that kinda talk right now. Rosie's not your anything. Good for you for growing a heart, but take that noise elsewhere."

I wanted to hug Kerdik, but knew that wouldn't go over

all too well. "Save the bickering for another time, guys. Kerdik, if you want to help because you want to keep Province 10 safe, whether or not I'm in it, then you can help us as much as you want. Aqueducts, fountain, all of it." I met his eyes to let him know I was about to hit him upside the head with some serious talk. "When Morgan's neutralized and Province 10 is stable, I'm going back to Common, and Bastien's coming with me. We're going to start a life together there. So make sure that your motivations have nothing to do with me, because sooner or later, I won't be in Avalon anymore."

Kerdik swallowed hard, and the room was so still, you could hear the bird on my shoulder's slight movements. "*If you leave with Bastien, I'll remain with Urien. As long as one of you is in Avalon, that's where I'll be. I'll not give up both the people I love. Faîte would suffer much if I didn't have daily reminders that there is still goodness in the world.*" His eyes flicked to Bastien with mild disdain. "When Bastien passes, come home to me. Then we can start your second life together. I'll make sure Avalon is a more peaceful place by the time you return to my arms."

Bastien rolled up his sleeves and cracked his neck twice. "That's it. You and me are taking this outside now. No magic, just us."

"Killing you would only speed up the time I get to spend with Rosie. I was willing to step aside and give you your life with her, but if you're giving me a pass, I won't say no to that."

My mouth fell open at the blatant machismo I couldn't stand. I let out a disgusted scoff and flipped my hair over my shoulder, not caring that I looked like a prima donna doing it. "Dudes, control your testicles. Stop acting like I'm someone to fight over. We're talking aqueducts, and that's all."

Bastien's gaze cut to Judah. "Do you need her here for this?"

I threw my arms into the air in exasperation. "This was my idea! I'm not going to be benched because you're in a mood to fight with Kerdik."

"I'm in a mood to end whatever hold you two have on each other," Bastien clarified, making the whole situation worse.

Kerdik waved his hand at Bastien, as if my boyfriend was a spider that annoyed him. "Go on and enjoy your time together. Take your dog for a walk, Rosie. Judah and I can figure out the rest."

"Call me a dog again, and see what happens!"

Judah's head bopped to the beat only the two of us knew. DMX was flowing through his veins when he shouted out his rap anthem that perfectly suited the moment.

No matter what, DMX could always center us, bringing us back to square one. During the great fight of where we would live off-campus, DMX had rescued us. Judah and I broke from the stupid argument Bastien and Kerdik were stuck in, and threw up our arms as we danced with our whole bodies and rapped together with obnoxious gestures, invoking the steps we'd made up during our many dateless nights, because we're both the shiz. Our grins couldn't be dampened as we squared off at the break, landing with gusto after a synchronized jump we'd practiced only about a hundred times. We slapped palms, and then knocked playful fists. We faced off and bent inward, our shoulders shaking to the beat and our feet stepping to the rhythm that would haunt us long after the song would end.

It was the perfect diffuser to the fight I couldn't have cared less about. Judah was always my good medicine. When the song ended, the two of us couldn't stop smiling. We threw our arms around each other and squeezed, breathing far easier, now that the other was within reach. "Normal life was so boring without you!" he admitted. "This one time, I saw an off-black Cadillac with the top back and windows down, and nobody said a thing!"

Of course, I started singing part of the hook from Mackelmore's "White Walls" song, because, duh.

Judah broke the hug and did a mimed thanks to Heaven. "See? That's why you're my best friend. Jill and everyone else just stared at me like I was a lunatic. I missed you so bad, Ro."

"You missed me? Dude, Avalon is bonkers. There's two men to every one woman here, so they all act like... I don't know. I'm not used to it. I miss my hump," I admitted.

"'My hump, my hump, my hump?'" His eyes were

sympathetic as he took in my form that was more womanly than it had ever been. "I see you, Ro. You're still in there."

Judah's stomach growled, which was a problem I could fix. "Come on. Let's go get something to eat." I motioned over my shoulder and turned my back to him to brace myself. "Hop on."

Judah didn't hop, since he was a few inches taller than me. He secured himself to my back, and I looped my arms around his thighs. The birds all landed on his back, chirping with amusement that they were getting a free ride, as well. I headed for the door, stopping short when Kerdik and Bastien both let loose incredulous shouts, telling us we couldn't walk through the halls like that.

"Oh, I super can. We do this all the time. My thighs are like tree trunks from years of indoor soccer. Judah's not a morning person, so this is how I got him to breakfast when we lived in the dorms freshman year."

Judah's chin rested atop my head. "You don't give Bastien a lift to lunch every day? Dude, you're missing out. Outsourcing transportation saves me so much time. I usually don't have to fully wake up until I'm actually at the table, which gives me an extra five or ten minutes of dozing. Best best friend in the world, right here."

Bastien guffawed at our candid nature. "I don't know what to do with this," he admitted, his expression torn between amused and irritated.

"Oh, that's alright. Go on back to yelling at each other. I

didn't mean to interrupt your fight. We'll be in the kitchen." I paused to jerk my chin up, silently asking for a kiss.

Bastien eyed Judah warily before moving in for a quick peck. "This is weird."

"No, this is Judah," I kidded, wanting to slap my knee at my lame joke. Judah compensated by letting out a hardy fake laugh to make me feel cool. I turned and hefted Judah further up on my hips, and stalked steadily toward the kitchen, away from the territorial tension.

29

FAMILY, SLATHERED IN BUTTER

After a week, Lane had healed enough for us to make public appearances. Damond's funeral was terrible. Though, I'm not sure what exactly might make for an awesome funeral. The Wildmen were supposed to play a song on their panpipes that increased reverence and peace, but somehow all we got were tears. I didn't feel a lick of tranquility through the whole thing, but instead wrestled with my inner turmoil that my cousin was gone, and I couldn't do anything to erase that harsh reality.

Remy, as usual, got nothing. He'd asked for nothing, other than to be granted permission to help me and my family. In the end, that was all life granted him, which was the biggest tragedy of all.

My family gathered by a tree in the courtyard, our heads bowed as we talked about our fondest memories of my healer. None of it made up for the fact that Remy was gone forever – my friend, my knight. We were a little quieter after that, but as the days passed, we were starting to figure out how to hold our heads up.

Dad, Lane, Draper and I managed to put together enough pieces of a smile to assemble a whole one for the newly christened Province 10. Lane barely breathed without Reyn hovering, making it clear that though she was recovering, he had not, and might not for a long time. I couldn't really blame him. I clung probably a little too tightly to her, too.

"I'm no doctor, but that Kerdik dude needs Prozac. He's straight up irritable," Judah remarked after a long day apart. I didn't like being separate from Judah, but he insisted he needed to be with Kerdik to make sure the measurements were perfect for the aqueducts they were installing. The whole process was shockingly simple when you had an immortal elemental going to bat for you.

Lane meandered around the kitchen, peeking in canisters to make sure she had all the ingredients. "A little? This is him calm. Before, when he and Rosie would go at it, his temper would shake the whole palace. Hazards of befriending a monster."

I frowned at Lane. "Kerdik's not a monster. He's a person."

"Actually, he's not a person, babe. Immortals aren't human."

"You know what I mean."

"I think it's precious that you're protective of him. He

doesn't have anyone besides Urien who sticks up for him, after all he's put Avalon through."

I raised my eyebrow at her, having a clear opinion about that. I didn't want to sound snotty, so I didn't point out that actually the Daughters of Avalon had inflicted most of the damage on the nation. "What are the beets for?"

"Food coloring."

"What are we making?" I partly whined. I loved surprises, but also grew impatient to open them. I hopped up on the counter, my jean-covered legs swinging back and forth beneath me, next to where Bastien was leaning. The bird on my shoulder fluttered from me to Bastien, and back again, asking what we were doing inside, when we'd been out all day in the Town Square with most of the province.

"You'll see, and you'll smile," she assured me.

Reyn's eyes tracked Lane wherever she meandered in the kitchen. She'd requested the space be left unstaffed for us that evening, and hadn't clued even Reyn in as to what her plans were. "I still don't understand what we're doing here."

"We're waiting for Draper and Urien. Then we're having some fun."

"Don't you all have court to hold tonight?" Reyn asked.

"We do, and we will. But we need some normalcy." She waved Draper and Urien into the kitchen when they appeared in the doorway. "Just in time." She raised her hands to Bastien, Reyn, Urien, Draper, Judah and me, and spoke loud enough for her voice to be the center. "Tonight, we're having some family time. This is a little something Ro, Judah and I used to do when we lived in Common. Once a week was family night. The rules of family night are as follows: No fighting. That's a hard and fast rule. Next is that we have to try something new. Cook a new recipe, go to a new place, meet new people – anything, but it has to be new. The final rule is that no one is too cool to get dirty and be goofy on family night. There are no adults, and no babies. We're all in, so respect the tradition."

I grinned as Judah started bopping his head to a beat I totally knew. This was part of Lane's magic that managed to carry over even into our life in Common. She could bring out the best in people – a skill not many possess.

Lane's eyes tinted with emotion as she pressed her hand to her heart. "When Rosie and I leave after Avalon's squared away, most of you are coming with us. When you do, this will be a little bit of what you can expect. Rosie didn't get a period of being gently broken in here. No one sat her down and explained all that was expected of her in Avalon, and it wasn't fair to her. If you come to Common with us, this is what we'll be doing. I hope you all come with us, and that we have decades of family nights together."

I beelined to Lane and wrapped my arms around her; I couldn't stop myself. This was the Lane I loved. No matter how many horrible things had happened, she still knew who she was, and I adored that about her. "I stinking love you."

"I love you, too, babe." She turned me around to face the room. "This is our new family. What do you think?"

"I think they need some breaking in." I remained attached to her, loving how strong we felt when we stood together. "What do you have in mind?"

"Thought I'd start out with something simple." She pointed to Bastien. "That one looks like he scares easily. How about making a little snack?" she suggested innocently.

The corner of Bastien's mouth lifted. "Hey, now. I already told you that I'm in this. I'm not so far removed from reality that I can't make a snack with you in the kitchen."

I returned his smile, relishing the breaking in Lane was about to do to all of them. "I think a treat sounds lovely, Lane."

Though Urien had told us all that he wasn't coming to Common with us, he and I hadn't put together enough memories yet. I was excited to make a few new ones with him and the rest of the crew.

Let me tell you a little story about making saltwater taffy: it's a full-body contact sport. It's not so much the measuring and boiling of the simple ingredients; it's the pulling of the taffy that got everything going. In no time at all, Draper, Judah and I were covered in butter and beet juice. It was the first time Draper actually laughed since news of Damond's death had muted his smile.

We were barefoot and slid all over the kitchen, giggling as we collided and fell, making every part of our bodies a slip-and-slide. Urien was more kingly in his neatness, only getting his hands greasy as he pulled taffy with Lane. The two couldn't stop laughing at the wrestling match Bastien, Reyn and I had fallen into, while Judah and Draper tried with all their concentration to pull the warm taffy without yanking each other around in a tug-of-war on the slick floor, which was now coated in a sheen of butter.

It had been a long time since I'd heard Reyn laugh, and the sound did all of us a world of good. He tripped over me and fell on Bastien, accidentally knocking the remainder of the beet juice from the counter, and dumping it on his own head. Red dye oozed all over Reyn and Bastien, who looked as though they were in a bloody deathmatch that had somehow devolved into boyish giggles. I tried to pull Reyn up, but slipped and collapsed with a squeak. I tried to stand, but I was so slippery, I only fell on him again, forcing out an "oof!" from us both.

After much finagling that looked a little like mild humping, Reyn managed to slither off of Bastien, who was still howling on the floor, holding his stomach as he fought with his levity for breath. I slumped over my boyfriend, holding him through our quaking chests and unbreakable grins. "Your hair looks amazing. I always wondered what you'd look like as a redhead."

"Oh, yeah? You think that's funny?" He reached down, slapping his hand in the puddle of beet juice. Securing my hips to his with an arm coiled around my waist, Bastien ran his red hand through my hair, leaving streaks of magenta and pink throughout. "Oh, that's a great color on you. Now we match."

I grinned down at him, basking in the glow of the familial feel of it all. With the invocation of family night, Bastien was officially mine, and I was very much his. "You're my boyfriend," I stated simply, gazing down at him with much unfettered affection.

Bastien looked at me, incredulous. "Is that just now dawning on you? I swear, woman. You drive me crazy."

"I mean, like, this is real now. You're part of our family."

Bastien's eyes met mine, and something serious passed between us while the kitchen was in full-on shenanigans mode around us. "This is what I want: the danger, the laughter – all of it. Whatever you've got, that's what I want in on."

There wasn't a thought in my head that contradicted the glow I felt for Bastien in that moment, and probably a thousand moments before this haphazard one. We were smeared with grease and dye, lying atop each other in the middle of the kitchen floor, but somehow, it was perfect. "I'm so in love with you, Bastien. This is all I want." My chest heaved with the aftershocks of laughter. I saw in him all the beautiful things that had led us to this haphazard slice of happiness. "Marry me," I blurted suddenly.

It was as if Lane's ears were attuned to my every breath, hearing me clear through the chaos. "What?" she shrieked, stopping mid-pull to gawk at me.

Bastien looked just as taken aback as Lane, but I didn't care. I wanted Bastien for a hundred thousand years, exactly like this – imperfect and completely precious. Passion and devotion blazed in his eyes as his arm tightened around my hips. His fingers traced my cheek, leaving streaks of butter down my face. "I'd marry you in any world, Daisy. Just say when, and I'm there. For the rest of my life, I'm there. Yes, I'll marry you."

30

COMING CLEAN WITH KERDIK

The hugs and congratulations that descended upon us were slick with sticky, greasy taffy, but nothing could have been sweeter. I had my family together, I was engaged, and they were happy for me.

The only way to cut through the slime that coated us from head to toe was a sponge bath of straight vinegar in the secluded back courtyard. It was well after the sun had set that Lane sent Judah to bed, with most of us grinning from ear to ear.

Except for me.

My smile fell when Bastien insisted that I tell Kerdik about our engagement. "You have to tell him tonight."

I shivered when the air hit my skin as I dressed behind the partition with Lane in the backyard. "Why does it have to be tonight?"

Lane fielded this one, throwing Bastien a bone.

"Because Kerdik's your friend, and getting engaged is good news. Why wouldn't you want to share that with your friend?"

I cast her a dubious look laced with probably too much attitude. "You know why."

Lane whispered so Bastien couldn't hear. "I don't look forward to Kerdik's temper when he finds out, but if this is what you want, then it's coming, whether you like it or not. Rip off the band-aid so the wound has time to heal. Kerdik's in love with you; no matter how long you wait, it's not going to be pretty."

My shoulders slumped as I threw my tank top over my head and pulled it down over my torso. Lane's movements were jerky and quick as she dressed, hiding her curvy and lithe body from the night, as if the darkness might sneak up on her from behind. I hated to see her glancing warily over her shoulder at nothing, and guarding her body when it was just us. As soon as she was dressed, I wrapped my arms around her and squeezed some comfort into her bones. "I love you," I stated simply. It was true; there was no girl I loved more than Lane.

She pulled back, tearing up at the mess her psyche had devolved into. Donning a brave smile that told me she was summoning as much grace as anyone could be expected to muster, she wiped her eyes and rolled her shoulders back. "I love you, too, baby."

"Are you alright?" Reyn called from the other side of the divide.

Lane grinned and rolled her eyes dramatically. "We're fine. Just braiding each other's hair." She grimaced. "Crap. Now we have to actually do that." She turned me around and started working on assembling two French braids down the sides of my head, her fingers working on muscle memory as twilight gave way to the night. When I turned around after she finished, she looked at me with a mix of confusion and pride. "You're engaged. My little girl's getting married. Are you sure about this? About him?"

"I can hear you, you know," Bastien harrumphed.

I nodded through my giggle and turned her around so I could braid her hair in the same fashion. "I am." Then I added to my volume so he could for sure hear me. "Bastien's too sexy for his shirt. So sexy, it hurts."

"That's more like it," he said, slightly mollified.

I snickered, and then lowered my voice. "Bastien's the guy for me, and I'm finally calmed down enough to where I feel like I can make that kind of decision."

"What about Kerdik?"

My shrug wasn't sincere. *What about Kerdik?* I hadn't figured out the enigma, nor what to do about our lingering connection. "Kerdik knows we can't be together."

"Knowing and accepting are two different things."

"I think this should be more of a silent trip to the salon tonight." I twisted her hair, tugging the two ends of the braids tight across the nape of her neck, and looping them up into the other side, so they made a sort of crown.

"Whatever you decide, I want your father with you

when you tell Kerdik about your engagement. He won't overreact if Urien's there to keep him calm."

"You act like Kerdik's a child. He can handle a little rocky news."

Lane turned around and gripped my shoulders. "Honey, I hope that's the biggest lie you've ever told yourself. Kerdik's got a toddler's temper. Acting like he doesn't is dangerous. Let him down gently."

I closed my eyes, wondering how many stupid choices I'd made to land myself here. "Tell me it'll all be okay. Tell me I'm not going to break the heart he just grew from scratch."

Lane didn't respond, but simply kissed my cheek and hugged me until I understood that it wouldn't be okay, but it was necessary. When she pulled back, it was with a determined gaze marring her smile. "Okay, then. Rip off the band-aid."

We were the last ones to be cleaned and dressed, and when we came out from behind the partition, Reyn heaved a gust of relief before he wrapped Lane in a tight hug. I wanted to tell him to ease up, but just like Lane, he'd been through enough to be able to act a little unhinged. If obsessive hovering was the worst he got, I couldn't fault the guy. Judging by the way she melted into his arms and drew a full breath, Lane didn't mind the extra affection.

Bastien was more controlled, his draw toward me understated for the viewers as he sifted his fingers through mine. Draper and Judah were whapping each other with towels, laughing as my dad chided them not to let Lane or me get snapped with an errant end. Judah responded by throwing two damp towels in Urien's face. My dad's look of shock was the best thing I'd seen in the last ten minutes, and made everyone laugh at the scandal. It had been a great evening, and I was a little sad that it was coming to an end.

"Alright, kids," Dad chided us. "To bed with Judah. Lane, Draper and Rosie, be ready to hold court with me in half an hour."

Judah stuck out his lower lip at being singled out. "Whatever. Rosie sleeps, too."

"So does Bastien now. Rosie will only sit with us for an hour before she goes to bed. I insist she continue her education on how to handle the problems of the people."

Judah stared at me as we walked up the stone steps that led to our bedrooms. "You have like, this normal family now. You have a mom and a dad. You even have a brother." There was a tinge of amazement, mingled with a note of jealousy. We'd always had just the two single moms in our corner.

I reached out and squeezed his hand. "So do you. That's what tonight was about. Lane and Urien belong to you every bit as much as they belong to me. Draper's your brother now. Plus, you're about to get a brother-in-law."

Bastien's chest puffed with pride. "We're getting married soon," he warned both Judah and me. I had a feeling that once our engagement went public, he wouldn't want to wait around to set a date. "Any brother of Rosie's is a brother of mine," he assured Judah with a firm nod.

"I'm super in love with you when you say things like that."

Bastien shot me a smirk. "I know."

I wasn't expecting Kerdik to be waiting for me in my bedroom, but there he was, wearing a proud smile at all he'd accomplished that day.

My lightness fell when I realized the heavy talk that was about to weigh us both down. Bastien shot me furtive glances as he helped Judah select a few things to borrow from his own wardrobe to take to the bedroom Judah had been given down the hall. Bastien wasn't totally keen on the two of us sharing a bed with Judah. I couldn't blame him, but it was a bummer nonetheless – a reminder that I was a grownup now, and sharing a bed with my bestie was probably weird at this age.

"How was your day?" I asked, starting out light as my hand fell out of Bastien's grip.

Kerdik beamed at me. "You should've seen the people working together. After Judah and I made the troughs, you all went into the castle while I moved them. The people came out and insisted on helping, even though I could've done it all myself. Someone even offered me a crust of bread when they took a break. One of the men, Pascal, shook my hand after we decided to call it quits for the night."

My heart tugged at the very normal things that Kerdik

had perhaps never been part of. He was used to working autonomously, and being feared by simply existing. "Being part of a team can be amazing. I'm so glad you had a great day, man."

"I did. We're about a quarter of the way done with the whole system's setup. I feel like that's pretty good."

"Pretty good? It's incredible."

"And how was your day?" He leaned in and sniffed my hair. "You stink like vinegar."

"Family night, per Lane's request. There's plenty of freshly pulled taffy downstairs. None of us wanted to eat it after we spent all evening making it. The cleanup wasn't all that fun, but I don't think the kitchen staff will off-with-my head in the morning."

"I should certainly hope not." He frowned and rubbed his chest, looking down at his shirt with concern.

"What's wrong?" Judah asked. I don't know why it surprised me when anyone was considerate to Kerdik. That Judah made an effort put things in a better light.

"Nothing, I think. Or something. I can't tell. I used a lot of magic today, so maybe that's it. I feel like something's off, but I can't put my finger on it."

"Well, that sounds ominous." My eyebrows pushed together as I frowned.

When my dad knocked on my door, I knew D-day had come. He cast me a let's-do-this look as he moved to sit in the chair in the corner of the room. "Bastien, why don't you show Judah to his new bedroom."

"Yes, your majesty." I often forgot that my dad was a big deal until his title was thrown around. Bastien touched my fingers before he left, though I wished he'd stayed (or that I'd left, and didn't have to deal with this mess).

Kerdik filled my dad in on everything that had happened during his day, talking animatedly with his hands, and smiling with pride at all he'd done for the province, while I took my sweet time changing into a loose gown for court. It was emerald, as most of my dresses here were, with rose-hued trim gusseting the low neck and the hemline. The capped sleeves were pink lace, and while the dress was pretty, I felt like it was missing a giant scarlet letter A across the swell of my breasts. When I came out with my stays undone, Kerdik made to tie them for me. He was always filling in the gaps where my knowledge or ability fell short, taking care of me without being asked. My heart ached at the thoughtfulness I knew I would soon be living without.

I stepped back from him with a tortured expression, my hand raised between us before he could fix my dress. "I... I have to tell you something." I couldn't bring myself to look at him, but stared at my feet instead as I toed on my gold sandals.

"Go on." Kerdik's smile fell when he saw my cagey glances toward my dad. "We'll be out in a minute, Urien."

My father slowly shook his head. "I think I'll wait here."

Though it was untied, my dress suddenly felt too tight.

My palms began to sweat as I paced, trying to find the right way to say the words that would break my green bestie's heart. "Dad, it's alright. I need to talk to Kerdik in private."

"No," Dad replied without apology or equivocation.

I swallowed a lump in my throat, still unable to look up at Kerdik. "Darling, what is it? Does Lane need my help? She was doing so much better this morning."

"I love that you love my family." I shook my head with my chin lowered. "I don't deserve how good you're being to us."

"I don't love your family; I love you." Then he nodded toward Urien. "And you." He reached out and took my hand in both of his, running his thumbs over my knuckles.

"I... I... I need you to take your ring back." I cringed, knowing that I would choose all the wrong words.

Kerdik's grip on my hand steeled. "I'm not taking back my gift. It's meant for you to wear."

My mouth went dry, and I feared the confession might remain stuck inside of me forever. It would take one sentence to crush him, and for the life of me, I couldn't get it out.

"Don't you like it? I thought you loved the look of your ring."

"I do! Kerdik, it's only the most beautiful ring I've ever seen in Avalon or Common. It's gorgeous, and you're wonderful for giving it to me. I can't wear it anymore, though."

"Tell me why," he demanded, his tone turning sharp.

My fingers were still winched in his grip, but I didn't try to wriggle free. Everyone was afraid of his temper, and I wouldn't add to that stigma.

"Because I... I can't wear it because..." I shifted and rolled my shoulders back, as the material of the dress started to make me itch. I wished for a black hole to open up and swallow me into its depths.

"Just say it!" The door banged open, and an angry gust of wind encircled us, creating a legit vortex that whirled a pair of my shoes and a few other items from the room around me. My hair whipped around my face, my eyes wide at the flare of his temper.

"Kerdik, you'll calm yourself down in front of my daughter!" Urien commanded, standing and bracing himself against the cyclone he was now on the outside of. "Rosalie, tell him!"

My dress flapped hard on my thighs, and despite everything, I leaned into Kerdik and wrapped my arms around him. Though he was the source of the chaos, I clung to him in hopes that he could shield me from the wind that tugged my dress to the side and loosened the ends of my braids. "Kerdik, you have to calm down! This is hard enough without a tornado in my bedroom!"

My dad was trying to get to me, but the wind separating us was too rough. "Kerdik, it's enough!"

"Tell me why you won't wear my ring!"

I was scared, not of him, but of the harm my words would do to him when they tumbled out of me in a rush. "I can't wear your ring because I've asked Bastien to marry me, and he said yes. I can't wear his ring and yours!"

Kerdik jerked my chin up, holding me tight to him so that my breasts were pressed to his chest. My hair swung out to the side, the wind keeping us in our own little world. "*You* asked *him*?"

"I did. We're going to be married." My eyes begged him to understand. "You knew this was coming."

"I thought I had more time! I thought you..." His expression turned a mix of frustrated, wounded and confused. "But I love you!"

"Kerdik, stop this wind! I can't think when you do crap like this."

The wind quieted, but didn't completely die. Still, I remained affixed to him, my chin cradled in his hand so that I couldn't turn away. My dad grumbled about Kerdik's temper.

Kerdik was in no mood. "Get out, Urien."

My dad crossed his arms over his chest. "Not while your temper's so unsteady."

"You all want me to be a person, but you won't grant me privacy during the worst conversation of my many lives? I'm not an animal to be put on display; I'm a man. I love your daughter, Urien, and she's marrying someone we both know isn't worthy of her."

"Are *you* worthy?" my dad questioned.

Kerdik sucked in a deep breath, and let it out as the

wind finally died around us. "Give us a few minutes to sort this out like adults."

When his voice seemed calm, my dad looked to me to gauge the situation. "Are you alright in here without me?"

I nodded with confidence, though my nerves were rattled. "Go on down to court. I'll see you there in a few."

31

THE TRUTH ABOUT THE DARKNESS

When my dad left, Kerdik locked the door behind him. "It was supposed to be me," Kerdik all but snarled. "Bastien's nothing like you. He's infatuated with you, which isn't the same as compatibility."

Despite the intensity of the moment, I scoffed. "How would you know? Bastien and me are good together."

"You two can't stay together for a month without breaking up."

Darn Kerdik and his valid points. "If that's true, then what are you getting so worked up about?"

Kerdik yanked me tight to him again, gripping me around the waist and making my heart race. "I don't want his ring on your finger!"

My glare met his, and despite how angry I wanted to get at him, I chose my words carefully. "It's not your choice.

It's mine, and I've made up my mind. I'm marrying Bastien, and you'll accept it."

"I've never wanted to snap anyone's neck more than his right now."

"Stop it with that kind of talk. You're supposed to want what's best for me."

"*I'm* what's best for you!"

"You want to talk about incompatible? You and I don't even have the same life expectancy."

"Neither do you and Bastien!"

Crap. I winced that he'd gotten in a second all-too-true point. "Why are you doing this to us? I don't want to lose you over what should be the happiest decision of my life."

"Make no mistake, marrying an Untouchable will be the worst decision of your life. I've been around for centuries, Rosie. I've seen how the men turn out who've managed to escape their armies. They can't calm down. They succumb to a vice that dulls the pain – alcohol, women, more fighting. They've got anger that runs deep. I don't want you married to that."

I shook my head, taking a few breaths to quell our fight. "Look, I wasn't naïve enough to expect you'd be happy for me, but we have to find a way to get somewhere stable with this."

"You love my ring."

I lowered my chin. "I do. But I love Bastien more than a piece of jewelry. I know it makes him uncomfortable – like you've got some claim on me." I rubbed the nape of my neck uncomfortably.

Kerdik's frustration lightened by degrees, and I saw a small smile curve the corners of his mouth. He reached his hand out and brushed over my shoulder the braids that had fallen to loose waves. "Where's the treachery in that? I thought you liked it when I claimed you."

My skin was practically crackling with the electricity I pretended I couldn't feel. I shouldn't feel it, but there it was – taunting me as Kerdik leaned in to brush his lips to my cheek. I felt the heat rise where his lips grazed, and knew that he'd seen the crime I couldn't deny in my blush. "I'm engaged," I reminded us both. "You shouldn't kiss my cheek like that."

"Like what? I'm just a friend of your father's, come over to pay your family a visit. You don't want me to kiss your cheek now?" His tone took on a scolding note, as if I was being ridiculous.

I shot him a baleful look. "You're making it sound dirty. Like you're an old man who's trying to seduce a teenager."

Kerdik's eyes narrowed, and I could spot his temper making its dreaded climb once again. "Did you ever seriously consider us? Or have you only ever had eyes for Bastien?"

I didn't know how to answer that. My hands were twisting in the fabric of my dress, and I couldn't look at him. "I don't think sparks like that fly from two people who've never considered the possibility of more. But it doesn't change that we shouldn't, and we can't. I love him, and you know it."

Kerdik nodded, and the silence that fell between us weighed heavy on my heart. "I think I'll leave the province for a while. Get myself some... something I can have."

Panic choked me around the throat at the thought of my... whatever Kerdik was to me, leaving. I knew it would be selfish to ask him to stay, but the confession bubbled out of me before I could access my higher reasoning. "I don't want you to go."

Kerdik shrugged, as if my words didn't pierce him. "I don't want to watch you marry someone else."

I chewed on my lower lip, willing my eyes not to mist over. "Here. You should have your ring back," I repeated, fumbling with my fingers to slide the treasure off my hand.

Kerdik caught my wrist and rolled my fingers into a fist. "No, darling. I have to... The ring isn't... You can't..." He exhaled his frustration. "You have to keep that ring on your finger, and not just because it would break the heart you gave me if you took it off." He ran his palm over his pressed pants, alerting me to his nerves. His eyes glanced to the lock on the door, and then he shot me an apologetic grimace when he stretched out his hand and raised up a stone wall out of thin air. I yelped in surprise, but trusted him enough not to totally freak out. The wall covered the door, closing us firmly in my room. He did the same thing to the windows, but when he saw my growing alarm, he moved his hand over the stone to make flowers appear on curly vines up the walls– as if that made it less of a prison. He turned the lantern up, but it was still dim, the atmosphere private and hushed.

"What's going on? Are we okay in here?" I fretted, glancing around warily.

"I have to tell you something, and I need you not to run out on me when I do."

I groaned internally. "Nothing good ever started with a preface like that. Out with it."

Kerdik took my quaking hands in his, turning on the bed so we were facing each other. He seemed older this way, more mature, as if he was about to break down the timeless secrets of the birds and the bees. "I don't know how much of my conversation with Brìghde made sense to you."

"About fifteen percent."

Kerdik leaned forward and brushed his nose to mine. It was a breath away from kissing, so I pursed my lips together, lest I tackle him with too much lust. "Tell me that you love me."

"You're killing me here. Out with it."

He brought my hands to his cheeks, so I was holding his face, his palms glued to the backs of my hands to keep me in place. "Long before you came to Avalon, things were different. There weren't just the Fae and Wildmen with innocuous abilities. Some could fly, others could turn invisible. The magic was stronger back then, which was sometimes a good thing."

"Okay, I knew a little bit about that. Bastien mentioned something like that a while back, and I think you or Lane, too."

Kerdik closed his eyes. "When you say his name, I begin to forget all the good you've shown me." He tilted his chin to the side to plant a kiss in my palm, reminding us both to be gentle. "Some of the magic still lingers, especially if you leave Faîte for a time and give yourself a chance to recharge. But overall, much of that higher magic is gone. It wasn't all good, mind you. Brìghde and Cailleach came to me with concerns that the moon was twisting some of the magic in their land. There were Fae biting each other, drinking blood to gain extra abilities – speed, strength, heightened senses, and things of that sort. Some of them were the type to lose their minds, seeking out only more blood, and more. We were worried that Éireland might devolve into chaos if the magic grew in its strength and continued to evolve as it had." He closed his mouth, gearing up to say his piece. I could tell that whatever he said next would be a doosie. He kissed my palm again to steady himself. "The three of us decided the magic was getting too hard to monitor. The people weren't using it for the greater good, but mostly to tear apart their land. I was worried about the twisted magic spreading to Avalon from Éireland, so we sort of took a little of it."

I tried to keep a level head, though I wanted to interrogate him right good. "You stole the magic from Avalon and put it in the nine jewels, right? Then you gave the jewels to my aunts and my moms."

"That's a good guess, and a popular one, but no. I took away the magic and kept it hidden from them. I took the excess and put it away. The blood drinkers, the Weres, and a few other creatures were slaughtered, and no more were born into the world. Faîte became a world of simple Fae, which made for less upset overall. That's when the people started to need me more often. Even nature needed me more often to maintain the land, so I made the nine gems for the Daughters of Avalon to sustain the land after the higher magic was taken." He rolled his eyes at the nature of life. "Morgan saw to upsetting the balance, of course, but I suppose nature has to find its way to revolt homeostasis somehow. That's neither here nor there, though. I took the higher magic and hid it for years until the tales of the chaos in Éireland fell to rumor and myth by the time they reached Avalon. Every year, I would move the stores of higher magic, so no one could find them and steal them from me. Trust me that Avalon wouldn't be able to handle power like that. The little I gave the Daughters – vitality, is all – they abused and fought over to the bitter end. I didn't have anyone to trust with the responsibility. If they knew what they held, it would surely corrupt the purest soul." He leaned forward and pecked my lips. "But then I met you. From the beginning, you were more concerned about me than you were about yourself. I'd never met anyone like you. I have a sixth sense about who I can trust, and I knew in the first five minutes that I could tell you all my secrets, and you would keep them as your own."

"Of course I would. I love you."

He closed his eyes to savor my words. "And I love you. It's why I knew I'd found someone I could truly trust. The higher magic is safely stored somewhere only I know." He cleared his throat and shifted on the bed, and I could tell he was nervous. I stopped breathing, worried that any movement might somehow rock the trajectory of the world too much. When Kerdik delivered the blow, I knew there was no bracing that could be done to steady myself against the blast. "I put all the higher magic – both the good aspects and the bad – into the ring that I gave you, so the people couldn't destroy themselves with it. Then I placed a binding charm on your ring, so that only you or I could remove it without severe consequences."

My hand froze on his face, and my whole body went stock-still. "I don't understand. This ring has Vampire and Werewolf magic in it? This is how people could get back their abilities to fly and go invisible?"

Kerdik nodded, contrite. "Among other things, yes. But they can't handle that kind of power. We can only intervene so many times before it's simply easier to take away the pot everyone's burning themselves on."

Panic gripped me around the throat as I rose up from the bed, tearing the ring off my finger. "Take it! I can't be trusted with that kind of power. What were you thinking?

What if I'd taken it off to bathe or something, and lost it? You seriously gave me a gigantic load of magic without telling me? What if Morgan figured it out? You could've made me her target, Kerdik!"

Kerdik stood and clamped his hand over my mouth. "The stone walls give us a little extra privacy, but they're not completely soundproof. Yes, I made a judgment call, and it was the right one. And you already were a target for Morgan, if you recall. She didn't need any prodding from your ring." He shook his head at the mess of it all. "Faîte would crumble if I restored their full magic to them. It would infect them like a virus, changing their makeup without their consent. People think I don't care what happens to Avalon, but I do. I was gone for so long because I needed to keep the dangerous magic away. It broke my heart to return and find that Morgan was abusing the little power I'd given her. The Jewels of Good Fortune were a test to see if I could trust any of them with the Darkness." He motioned to my ring, letting me know that the beautiful gem he'd given me had a name associated with horror.

"My ring is called the Darkness?" I shivered at the indication of doom.

"That's one of the things that's locked inside, yes. Lane and Tyronoe passed the test. They gave their jewels back to me when they saw all the destruction that was happening between the sisters. Then Tyronoe was killed, and Lane left Avalon to take care of you, so again, there was no one except for me who could be trusted to keep the higher magic from infecting the land."

My mouth fell open beneath his palm. So many people assumed Kerdik didn't have a soul, but I knew better. To fathom his heart breaking over the downfall of Avalon still surprised me, though. "This Cailleach woman, what if she decides one day she wants the magic back? Secrets like this always come out. What happens then? Will she come after me? I can't defend myself against an immortal!"

"She can't kill you. Only a Daughter of Avalon can murder a Daughter of Avalon. You can't die from her hands, but only by the hands of an animal, natural causes, or time." He gripped the back of my head and pulled me forward, so our foreheads were pressed together. "And I've given you more time, plus extra power to heal from the errant animal attack. Cailleach doesn't want the higher magic roaming about the world any more than I do. She'll not come after you, darling."

I closed my eyes, feeling his breath fan across my nose. "What about Morgan? I don't want what happened to Lane with those terrible soldiers to happen to me. If Morgan finds out..."

Kerdik thumbed my lips that were malleable to his call, despite my aching conscience. "I saved you from that attack, didn't I? I would never let that happen to you, my love. I'll always come for you."

"You have to take the ring back."

Kerdik shook his head, his forehead mashing to move

my head in time with his. "It's not safe with me. There are times when I want more power than I have, more dominance. My self-control has lasted as long as I can expect it to. For so long, I needed someone to help me carry this burden. Then you came along, and I knew I'd met the one person I could trust with the awfulness of the world. You would be gentle with it, because you were gentle with me."

Kerdik's shoulders did seem weighted at mention of the long journey that had led to him putting the ring on my finger. "Hey, I'm here. This is a horrible thing to have to guard for so long." I swallowed hard. "I can help you."

His gust of relief bathed my nose. "Thank you. When I argue with Cailleach and Brìghde, part of me is tempted to set the magic loose, to let their people destroy each other just to get them to cooperate."

"Cooperate with what?"

Kerdik's fingers migrated to my shoulder, fingering the lace as if he wanted to slide it off so he could suck on the skin beneath. "I want to make love to you. More than anything, I want to be with you in every way a man can. Every day they don't remove my curse, it's a day I'm tempted to set their dark magic loose. I want them to feel impotent. I want them to feel alone in the mess as their land collapses in fits of chaos."

"Shh," I cooed, trying to soothe the tumult I could feel rising up in him. "You're not alone, honey."

"You're marrying Bastien," he countered flatly, retracting his touch from my sleeve.

"Yes, I am." I was firm on that point, even through my attraction for Kerdik.

"Tell me you'll save your second life for me." He grimaced and shook his head. "That's not how I should've asked." Kerdik shocked me to my core when he stood us both up from the bed, and then slid down onto the floor on bended knee before me. He awakened parts of my heart that shouldn't be available for poking at when he blinked up at me with rapture and vulnerability shining through.

Confusion tugged the corners of my mouth downward, and my palms started to sweat. "What are you doing?" I began to give way to panic at the unnatural position we were in. "You shouldn't kneel. People kneel to you, not the other way around."

Kerdik looked up at me through thick lashes with purpose and poise. "Rosalie Avalon, I'll love you with all of my many lives. When I saw your kindness, I knew the true scope of your beauty. Before you, I was..." He swallowed, and we both knew just how lost he'd been before our friendship anchored him to something real. "Now there's someone worth returning to, worth fighting for."

I couldn't make sense of the grand nature of it all. There's something about a man on bended knee that makes you feel simultaneously powerful and scared. It's too many cards to hold. I swallowed thickly, my veins filling with trepidation and attraction. "Kerdik, get up."

"No," he countered with a challenge to his tone. He remained kneeling before me – the most powerful creature in all of Avalon. "Let me do this. No matter the outcome, I need to get this out." He took my jeweled hand and placed it over his heart. "It's you, darling. It's always been you. When your first life is over, will you take me as your husband?"

My heart was the only sound I heard as I gaped, utterly flabbergasted at him asking instead of demanding. Though this wasn't the time to love him, I did. Oh, how I cherished the enigma that was Kerdik. Part of me knew that no matter how long I lived, I wouldn't outgrow him, and couldn't turn my heart off when he looked my way. Even if we could never make love, I still wanted to be his, and for him to be mine all mine.

I leaned over so I could stroke Kerdik's lips with my thumb. It was a simple blessing that took us to a sweeter place than the desperation-filled air that dragged in and out of our lungs. "I promise."

Kerdik exhaled with a grin that was so beautiful, I couldn't look away. "You'll marry me?"

"Not in this life, but in the next. Yes." He stood and wrapped me in a hug, his chest swelling with joy. I stepped back, knowing we'd carried on enough. "We can't indulge in anything right now, though. This was our goodbye. You have to let me live this life with Bastien."

Kerdik's mouth hardened into an angry line. "Don't say his name to me."

One of us had to break the cycle. I moved toward the center of the room, putting a few feet of distance between us. "It'll be easier when I take him to Common with me. You won't have to see us together. The higher magic – all of it will be gone where it can't hurt Faîte anymore. *I* won't be able to hurt you anymore, either. Easy-peasy."

Kerdik stood and straightened his vest. "None of this is easy, Rosie. Now if you'll excuse me, I'm going to get back to work setting up the aqueducts."

I blinked at him in surprise. "You're staying to help us?"

"You say that like you think I don't care if my future bride has access to water or not. I care, darling. Even when you're not mine yet, I care." He was tall and leonine, standing before me like a man ready to take charge and make the world his own.

Selflessness was a trigger for me, activating my ready-to-pounce button I wished Kerdik didn't have access to. I took another step back to counteract my libido.

I was about to tell him how not worth all of this I was, but a sudden rumbling under my toes stopped me short. I narrowed my eyes at him. "Knock it off, dude. You can't go bringing down the house like this."

Kerdik's wary expression gave me pause as his eyes darted around the room. "That's not me."

I took a few steps back as the trembling built up to a full-on earthquake. My heart started to thump unevenly as my hand shot out to steady myself against the stone wall. "If not you, then who?"

Panic shot through me when Kerdik grabbed his chest and howled, dropping to his knees as though he'd been shot straight through the heart. I ran to his side, scooping up his torso in my arms. "Kerdik! Honey, what's happening?"

He tried to say something to me, but could only mouth his fear. He clung to me, his eyes wide with sudden pain.

Terror raced through my veins as I held him, wondering what could possibly take down the most powerful being in all of Avalon.

Love the book? Leave a review.

I feel like you know by now I have no qualms killing off your favorite characters if you don't leave a review online. I know how attached you are to Link.

32

STUBBORN GIRL

Here's a free preview of *Stubborn Girl*,
Book 7 in the *Faîte Falling* series.

If anyone ever thought to put together a manual about what to do if an immortal had a full-blown heart attack out of nowhere, I would read that book. Or, more accurately, I'd have someone else read it to me.

Kerdik grasped his chest as I held him on the floor of my bedroom, panting in confusion and fear. It was the latter emotion that clinched in my chest. Kerdik wasn't supposed to be afraid of anything. What hope was there that any of us could stand against something that scared the most powerful being in all of Avalon?

My emerald dress was pooled on the floor around us as

I clutched him tight. When his breathing started to even out, I nearly cried from the relief. "Honey, what is it? Kerdik?" I ran my hand over his chest, hoping to calm either one of us.

"Rosie?" he whispered, his eyes wide and worried.

"What happened? We were talking, then the palace started shaking, then you grabbed your chest like you were having a heart attack, and now... What? Are you hurt?"

I didn't know how much more weird Avalon stuff I could handle. Kerdik had just admitted to me that the ring he'd put on my finger when we'd first met held all of the lost magic in Faîte – both the good stuff and the bad. The ability to turn Fae into Vampires and werewolves had been locked away, along with other, less devastating magic, like the ability to fly or turn yourself invisible. The higher magic had been locked away when it was clear it was doing more harm than good. No one knew what became of it, except for Kerdik, who'd been waiting for someone he trusted to come along. All this time, an atomic bomb of magic had been perched on my ring finger.

"Something's happened to..." Kerdik's pupils flicked from side to side in alarm. He appeared as though he was seeing a scene far away that I couldn't witness.

And then suddenly, I could. Kerdik was in distress, so our connection made me see what he saw. The first time this happened, I'd seen through his eyes. Now it seemed I was seeing the world through his mind's eye.

Brìghde was on all fours, teeth gritted as she clutched

at the stone floor of a dungeon with her mannish hands. Her pale skin and red hair were filthy. Her dress looked like it was pure earth – made of moss or something – and it was torn at the hem up to her knee. Her face was burned, but worse than pain, one of her cheeks and her forehead were now disfigured. The puckered and shiny skin was immoveable as she spoke. "Ye don't know what you've done, mortal! Once I break free of whatever it is you've got tha's holding me, I'll take my time tearing ye apart. What-ever protection ye have tha kept me from killing ye, I'll find a way around, make no mistake."

The focus shifted upward, and I saw before I heard the cruelty of my birth mother. Morgan le Fae was standing over Brìghde with a sneer that looked well-prac-ticed. She wore a red satin gown with no bustle, her chocolate-colored hair tied up in a crown of braids. Her pinched nose matched mine, though her face looked so murderous, I wished none of my features matched hers. "That was a nice little surprise. I can't be killed by an immortal, eh? Why, if only I'd known earlier. The fun I could've had." She kicked Brìghde in the ribs, and Brìghde exhaled a puff of black smoke. "Now, summon him."

"I wouldn't wish you on Kerdik, and I wish a fair many grave depravities on him. Summon him yourself."

Morgan picked up the hat Kerdik had given me to wear back when we'd first met. When I'd been thrown into the well, my belongings had been left in Morgan's castle, leaving the Newsies cap up for grabs. "I've got a token from him, so you can use that to call him here."

"Call him yourself!"

"Why my acid doesn't control your will, I can't understand. At least your abilities have been weakened. I can't be killed by you, but I wonder if *you* can be killed by *me*?"

Kerdik and I both shouted for Morgan to stop when she set down the hat on the floor of the dungeon and picked up a knife. Our cries were ineffectual as Morgan picked up Brìghde by her hair and stabbed her through the chest.

Brìghde's howl had a hawk-like shriek to it, making my spine tingle. For a moment, she went limp, and Morgan released her to slump to the floor. I called out her name, but we were on opposite ends of the country. I could hear pounding and shouting, but those noises were in my immediate reality – no doubt Urien or Bastien realizing we were walled inside the bedroom, and trying to bust through the thick stone. Some people just lock the door when they want a little privacy, but not Kerdik. He'd erected stone to cover the door and window, so we could have a few moments uninterrupted.

I hadn't been expecting him to propose – to ask instead of demand I spend my second life with him. Neither of us expected me to say yes, but here we were, trapped in my bedroom while the world fell to pieces.

Brìghde began to stir, and my heart nearly stuttered. I didn't know Brìghde, but her lifeline was the same eternal circle as Kerdik's. If something could kill her, it might take him down, as well. Brìghde coughed out a raspy, "Harder next time, ye rotten bitch."

"Oh, I can make it hurt far worse than that."

"Pain doesn't mean the same to an immortal as it does to ye. Even what you've done to my face will heal."

"That would be true, if I didn't have pools more of it, ready to dowse you as soon as you get your bearings back. I'll have you here for as long as it takes to get what I need."

"Ye can't have it. It's a myth. I can't make ye immortal."

I paled, wishing anything else had come from her mouth. Morgan somehow knew about my extended lifespan now. She knew, and she wanted. It was the ultimate power – to remain on her throne forever, to be the second immortal to reign over Avalon.

Morgan's fist shook around her bejeweled dagger. "I know that Rosalie's immortal now! Only Kerdik, you or Cailleach could've made her that way, and I know it was Kerdik. He turned fool for her long ago." She stabbed Brìghde through the back, puncturing her lung. Her fury made it seem like she wasn't just angry at Brìghde, but that she meant the knife for me, whom she couldn't get at. Morgan spoke above Brìghde's gasp and scream. "If he can turn Rosalie immortal, then you can grant me that same favor! Do it, or your long life will be spent in my dungeon, howling like an animal." When Brìghde couldn't answer because of her punctured lung, Morgan huffed, as if her prisoner was being annoying on purpose. She tapped her foot impatiently as she waited for the wound to heal enough for their tumultuous back and forth. "I must warn you; if you don't give me what I need, I'll trap Kerdik here next. Don't think I won't do it. I'm not afraid of him!"

Only I knew how very untrue that declaration was.

Don't leave a girl hanging!
Start Stubborn Girl today.